The Winter in Anna

also by Reed Karaim

If Men Were Angels

The Winter in Anna

a novel

Reed Karaim

W. W. NORTON & COMPANY
Independent Publishers Since 1923
NEW YORK • LONDON

Printed in the United States of America
First Edition

For information about permission to reproduce selections from this book,
write to Permissions, W. W. Norton & Company, Inc.,
500 Fifth Avenue, New York, NY 10110

For information about special discounts for bulk purchases, please contact
W. W. Norton Special Sales at specialsales@wwnorton.com or 800-233-4830

Manufacturing by Quad Graphics Fairfield
Book design by Fearn Cutler de Vicq
Production manager: Anna Oler

Library of Congress Cataloging-in-Publication Data

Names: Karaim, Reed, author.
Title: The winter in Anna : a novel / Reed Karaim.
Description: New York : W.W. Norton & Company, [2017]
Identifiers: LCCN 2016027495 | ISBN 9780393608502 (hardcover)
Subjects: LCSH: Journalists—Fiction. | Man-woman relationships—
Fiction. | GSAFD: Love stories.
Classification: LCC PS3561.A5745 W56 2017 | DDC 813/.54—dc23 LC
record available at https://lccn.loc.gov/2016027495

W. W. Norton & Company, Inc.
500 Fifth Avenue, New York, N.Y. 10110
www.wwnorton.com

W. W. Norton & Company Ltd.
15 Carlisle Street, London W1D 3BS

1 2 3 4 5 6 7 8 9 0

This is for Lisa.

The Winter in Anna

Chapter 1

THERE ARE LIVES THAT END BADLY. Hers was one of those. I would like to pretend that isn't true, but I can't. So this is how Anna's life ends. On a night sometime late in winter, in an anonymous motel somewhere in the Midwest, she sat down on the edge of the bed and drank a quart of bleach, irreparably burning her esophagus and her stomach and dying alone and quite painfully. I can't change this, and I can find no honest way to make it sound less terrible than it was.

There was one other thing the friend who called with the news told me.

"She left the door open." He hesitated, confused. "I guess she wanted to be found. Maybe she was hoping someone would stop her."

"I suppose," I said, but I didn't think that was it at all.

"I mean, why would you do that, if you didn't want somebody to see you and stop you?"

"I don't know," I said, but I was picturing the door half open, the parchment light of the winter moon framed like a formal invitation, maybe even snow falling in a familiar, seductive whisper, and I did know.

Knowing was the hardest part. After we hung up I rode the elevator down to the lobby and walked over to Pennsylvania Avenue, where the midday sun washed out the world briefly, mercifully. I sat down on a bench on Lafayette Square and I can't say what I felt at first. A distant sense of absence. A loss, yes, but almost abstract, a feeling some part of my past had been reordered, as if I had just found out that a treasured memory was not as I had remembered.

Oh, Anna, I thought, you almost made it to another spring.

And in the simple act of clearly forming her name—Anna, that unadorned, oddly balanced teeter-totter of a name—sorrow came crashing down, and it wasn't distant or abstract at all. I could see her so clearly it took my breath away. No one had been more alive to my younger self. No one had held the bright possibility of existing fully in each day more than she had. No one had seemed to defy the idea that our future is written in our past more than Anna. Our time together filled my mind, and what I remembered was not a surrendered life.

But the open door was still there, and with it the possibility I had been wrong about everything. Years later and I still don't know. So I've decided to write this. I will tell you Anna's story, and you tell me if I have written a tragedy.

Chapter 2

I MET ANNA WHEN I WAS TWENTY, and I was her friend, or whatever you decide to call it, for a little more than a year. Also, during most of that time, her boss. We were working at a weekly newspaper in a small town in central North Dakota. The town of Shannon was positioned at the spot in our national geography where the Midwest becomes the West: distances expand, the sky gains dominance over the earth, and the wind arrives unimpeded from beyond the sere edge of the world, a herald of how vast and empty it really is.

The Shannon Sentinel had a full-time staff of three, the editor, the assistant editor, and the sports editor, along with a collection of older women who performed part-time jobs. It was run by Art and Louise Shoemaker, the couple who owned the print shop in back, which was the part of the business that actually made money.

I had taken the job as the sports editor after dropping out of college one semester short of graduating. My last act on campus had been to tear the phone number of the *Sentinel* off an advertisement for the job pinned to the bulletin board of the university newspaper, where I had been working as a student editor. My inability to finish school so close to the end was the result of the distraction caused by a girl, who had realized quite correctly that she would be better off without me, and a host of lesser factors, not the least of which was that I had grown up on college campuses—my parents were both teachers—and it suddenly felt intolerable that I should spend one more day in the company of the stately red brick, manicured lawns, and vaguely indolent springtime air of the state university, where I had more or less stopped attending classes anyway.

So I drove out to Shannon and, blessed with the confidence that comes from not caring, got the job. The town had 4,532 people, a factory on the edge of town that manufactured bomb parts for a multinational corporation headquartered in Dallas, towering silver grain elevators along the railroad tracks, and, in a nondescript one-story brick building on the far end of Main Street, the office of *The Shannon Sentinel*.

The "newsroom" was in front, visible through a plate-glass window to anyone wandering down the sidewalk. It wasn't much of a newsroom, three metal desks pushed together in the center of the room, another two along the wall. There was a counter by the door, as if we were a dry cleaner's or a bait shop, and when someone came in, one of the older women stood up and took their classified ad or announcement of the Knudson or Payne family reunion, or simply stood and chatted about the day's news, which often seemed to be the only point of the visit.

I had one of the desks in the center of the room, but during my days as the *Sentinel*'s sports editor (and only actual sportswriter) I spent little time at it. My job was to cover the high school teams in the county, and I worked mostly at night. I'd taken an apartment above a bank, two blocks from the paper, that had once been a doctor's or dentist's office. You entered through a narrow hallway that led to the other rooms, each behind a heavy wooden door with a frosted glass window, on one of which you could still faintly make out the name of Dr. Neil Epstein. I had a bedroom, a bath, and a living room/kitchenette with a sink, stove, and a few cabinets along the inside wall. Oddly enough, the apartment had no refrigerator.

Large old-fashioned casement windows looked out on the Buffalo Bar across Main Street. The bar's red neon sign, the name written in cursive letters intended to look as if they had been formed by a lasso, reflected faintly along the bottom of the windows in both the bedroom and living room. The rest of the street was desolate at night, plate glass and locked storefronts, the empty sidewalks the dull gray of a worn tombstone.

The bar was where I ended up eating most evenings. I knew no one in town and it was often late when I got home. There was a pool table in back, and I played one of the old men who seemed to live at the Buff, and went back to my apartment sometime before closing. I wasn't actually old enough to drink legally in North Dakota, but they knew I was working for the newspaper and nobody thought to ask.

I have slept poorly or not at all since I can remember. As any insomniac can tell you, there is a perfect stillness and sense of emptiness that comes very late, when you have worried about all the things you can worry about, when the house has settled in for the night and even the stray barking dog has given up and is balefully eyeing the duplicitous moon, a moment when the universe collapses into simpler forms, the pillow beneath your head, the warmth of an old quilt, the faint play of light along the ceiling, which at three a.m. can assume the shape of almost anything.

Now I am a married man, with my wife beside me and a young daughter asleep in the next room, and I lie silently and very still, letting my dreaming wife and child believe their world is at rest. Now it's easy to wait out the night, but when I was young I couldn't stand to lie in bed with the possibility that the blank screen of the ceiling would start to show me movies I didn't want to see. I was only twenty years old, but in the darkness my life already felt filled with a vague sense of failure, as if I had missed some intersection along one of North Dakota's razor-straight roads that I should have seen coming long in advance, so I often stayed up reading or just sitting in the dark.

The best thing about my apartment, the reason I had taken it despite the absence of food-cooling apparatus, was the windows looking out on Main Street. After coming home from the bar I sometimes stood in front of them and rested my forehead on the cool glass, watching the deserted street with a strange feeling of expectation, as if, should I wait long enough, I'd surely see something that would explain why I was here. I often tugged over the beat-up blue chair that came with the apartment and rested my feet on the sill. After a while I felt as transparent and insubstantial as the glass, and this was a solace, a kind of peace, even if I was still afraid to lie down until dawn appeared above the flat-topped mercantile buildings across the street.

I'd met Anna by then, probably on my first or second day

on the job, but she had registered only as this dark-haired, slender, silent, and somewhat furtive woman, pretty, perhaps, but hard to say, one of those people who seem to be always sliding out of the edge of your vision. We would like to think we will recognize the people who come to matter to us at first sight, but of course that's absurd. They often slip into the corners of our lives, unnoticed, then taken for granted, until one day, if we are lucky, we see them anew with startled comprehension, and think, *There is my best friend*, or *There is the woman I love*, or *There is someone who saved me*.

The truth is, I didn't think about her—I didn't think much about anyone at the newspaper—until the day in Shannon that my future arrived in the form of an obituary.

Chapter 3

"THIS CAN'T BE GOOD," is the first thing I remember Anna saying.

She had a soft voice, often barely above a whisper, but wine-dark and burred along the edges, the voice of someone who smoked a pack a day of Marlboro Lights and drank way too much coffee. Even then, she was quietly pursuing her poisons.

I was at my desk trying to finish a story on the regional track meet. I looked through the window to see a half dozen somber-looking middle-aged men and one woman marching down the sidewalk toward the door.

"Who's that?"

"The entire city council," Anna said with the tone of someone observing an unusual flock of migrating birds.

They marched in, past us and into Art Shoemaker's office in the back of the room. The murmur of discontented voices leaked through the wall.

I had staked out a privately held position that there was nothing in Shannon I would ever care about and that my responsibility for the community's welfare ended with correctly tallying box scores. Still, I couldn't help myself.

"What's going on?"

Anna sat at her typewriter with her fingers on the keys, wrists very straight, excellent secretarial school form. She had finely sculpted features and a compact, attractive figure, and all that registered in the back of my mind, but I wasn't sure I remembered her name. It was either Anna or Sarah or maybe Myra.

"I imagine it has to do with the error," she said.

"The error?"

"There was an error in the story on the council meeting Tuesday."

The story had been written by our editor, Stacy Reynolds, who was only a couple of years older than I was, but who had managed to graduate from a journalism school in Minnesota and who spent most of her time trying to sleep with the county's buffed-out deputy sheriff. His exploits had been on the front page three out of the last four issues, which was a feat, since the last recorded crime to go beyond a juvenile misdemeanor in Shannon had happened before I'd joined the staff. The most recent photo of him standing front and center, muscled arms across his broad chest while, in the background, blurred high school students filed outside for a fire drill, seemed particularly gratuitous.

Stacy was out now, sleeping in. Perhaps last night had been the night.

"So—what error?"

"A number. Almost nothing, really." Anna's eyes widened slightly. "Literally, nothing. An extra zero."

"An extra number? In what?"

"The cost of the city repaving project. It went from seven million to seventy million dollars."

Three hours later I was in back, in the pressroom, wasting time with Todd, the younger of the two printers, when I felt a hand on my shoulder.

Louise Shoemaker was standing too close, as she always did. Louise was tall, taller than her round and soft-faced husband, with square shoulders and a long, strong jaw that made her look like an unnerving cross between Eleanor Roosevelt and Burt Lancaster. But the jaw was nothing, really. Her left eye was the thing. It was bloodshot, perpetually and completely bloodshot, a kind of fiery red collapsed sun. There was something wrong with it, but no one at the paper had ever had the nerve to ask what.

When she was standing close, the most important thing was not to look at her eye, and yet it was impossible. You're *supposed* to look someone in the eye—not one eye, of course—but there you were, trying to be polite and look Louise in the eyes, *both* eyes equally, and there was this one ordinary eye, possibly a light gray or blue, and this other eye, this miniature stellar phenomenon, with swirling depths and odd veins and pools of blood-red light and a terrible gravity tugging at you.

I usually tried to look at the point just above her nose and directly between her eyes, which left me feeling slightly cross-eyed and meant Louise was never quite in focus.

"How are you, Ricky?" She was a woman of bottomless heartiness. "Are you having *fun*?"

It was her favorite question, one she asked almost every time she saw me.

"Absolutely."

"It's *supposed* to be fun, you know."

"It is. *Absolutely*."

"Good. We need a new editor."

My gaze slipped and I was staring into her about-to-go-nova eye, and I felt myself falling through space and time, perhaps even experiencing interdimensional travel.

"It'll be a lot of *fun*!"

"Stacy—"

"Stacy makes too many mistakes, Ricky. She makes mistakes with names. She makes mistakes with numbers. Do you know we've never had a *single* complaint about the box scores this entire basketball season? I can't remember the last time that happened!"

She said this with such a flourish of appreciation, I felt I had balanced the federal budget or solved one of the world's great mathematical puzzles. My vision slid over her shoulder and I saw Anna standing by the door to the newsroom. I had no idea how long she had been at the paper, but I knew it was longer than I had.

"What about . . . Anna?" I asked, taking a stab at the name and a silent breath of relief when it appeared I was right.

"No, no, no, she's happy where she is. Come on, it'll really be fun!"

Anna was still, but our eyes met and I thought I saw a brief brush of gratitude.

"I've been thinking about going back to school," I said.

I hadn't, but in the face of real responsibility, it suddenly seemed like a good idea.

Louise leaned closer. "If you can't do it, Ricky, I'm going to have to take over myself. I'd like to stay retired, but if I have to get behind a desk again, well, we'll just have a *great* time!"

Louise had once been a hell-raising reporter at the daily paper in Fargo before marrying Art, the small-town print shop owner, and becoming the editor of the *Sentinel*, in those early days knocking back bourbons and water at lunch before settling in to bat out denunciations of the *petit bourgeoisie*, *le imbéciles de conservateurs de commerce*—editorials that left the town's civic leaders both shell-shocked and searching the municipal library for French dictionaries.

It seemed possible Louise had been drinking heartily this noon. Behind our boss, Anna was shaking her head, slowly but firmly, side to side.

"I don't know," I said. "I need to think about it."

. . .

I WENT OUT to the municipal golf course to avoid thinking about it. In early April the flags weren't up on the greens and the grass was still a pale, winterish brown. A thick fog had risen after a late morning rain and there was no one else on the course. I hit my ball off the first tee into an earthbound cloud as I heard a car pulling up behind me.

I turned to see Todd rolling down the window and looking uncomfortable.

"There's been an accident at the railroad crossing. Art asked me to get you."

"How did you find me?"

Todd was wiry, with a shock of straw-colored hair and skin

as pale as newsprint from his long days in the windowless back shop. He had a tattoo of Wile E. Coyote on his left bicep and a ghost of a mustache he had been working on since I'd arrived in town.

"There's like five places you could be, man. I checked your apartment first."

Rain had started to congeal out of the fog. I could see my breath.

"So, anyway, with you being the new editor—"

"No. I haven't decided yet."

Todd shrugged. He didn't like to offend anyone.

"Well, I guess you're as close as we got right now. You want me to find your golf ball?"

. . .

THE RAILROAD TRACKS bisected the town, east to west, with thirty feet of stone slag on each side creating a dead zone that ran through the heart of Shannon. On Main Street a pair of crossing guards, with the usual red lights that flashed when descending, marked the intersection. The guards were down and the lights were flashing as I pulled up. A train was nowhere to be seen, but the city ambulance and the sheriff's car were parked west of the tracks, the fire engine on the other side, with a city police car next to it.

Men from the volunteer fire department were walking up and down the rails in the rain, which was falling steadily now. They walked in pairs, staring at the gravel ahead of their feet, and every once in a while someone stopped and reached down to pick up something obscured by the gauze of fog and rain.

They all wore green rubber gloves, and the day seemed to have no color but for the industrial green of the gloves, which reached up to their elbows and unnerved me for some reason that floated just beyond my comprehension.

"He sat down on the tracks." The deputy sheriff had come up beside me. "They never even saw him. They were two miles outside of town when they radioed back and said they thought they might have hit something. It took them another mile to get the train stopped. Mac's out there now, talking to them."

Day and night, coal trains moved through Shannon, hauling lignite from the huge open-pit mines on the edge of the badlands to Minneapolis–St. Paul and on to the furnaces and mills of Ohio, Illinois, and Michigan, the great Midwestern engine of the nation. The trains were more than a mile long and moved with the gravity and momentum of planetary systems. If you were out in the country you sometimes saw them bisecting the world, an endless string of open cars, each with a dull black hump rising at the center, as if the crust of the earth were being shuffled west to east. When they came through town they could stop traffic for ten minutes. They never slowed down more than required by law and as soon as the engines cleared city limits they sped back up, the cars in the back rattling by in blurred succession like the frames of an out-of-focus film. I could easily believe it had taken them a mile to stop. Even after hitting someone.

"Who was it?"

Rain dripped off his hat. His eyes were young and confused. "Tom Lund."

He could tell I'd never heard of him.

"Old guy. Retired. Think he might have a daughter or something in town."

I walked down to the siding, feeling the stones beneath my feet, a line of low sheds or small warehouses on the far side of the tracks decomposing in the rain. The rest of Shannon had vanished, leaving this nowhere land of rock and rain and men trudging with their heads down, as if they had been sentenced to march along these glistening rails disappearing into the distance for some crime that still shamed them. One of them was Paul Strand, the senior printer at the paper, middle-aged, with gray eyes and a flat businesslike face. I knew he was some kind of officer in the volunteer fire department but I'd never seen him outside the office before. He nodded, as if it was right I was there, and went back to staring at the siding along the tracks.

He took a step and stopped. He bent down and lifted something the color and composition of day-old steak but larger, the size of a forearm. The man walking with him averted his eyes and opened a heavy green trash bag. Paul dropped the thing in the bag and looked at me. He wasn't wearing a hat, and rain ran down his face and dripped off his chin.

"There's pieces of him all along here." He nodded at the tracks disappearing into the rain. "You get hit by a train . . ."

He shrugged at the absurdity of it, or the sadness, or maybe just the misery of the job. I fell in beside him as he walked with his partner along the tar-black wooden ties protruding at right angles from rails polished as bright as new coins by the trains. The siding, rising toward the tracks, was angled and uneven, the stones damp. I walked carefully, afraid of what might appear beneath my feet, trying to see each and every stone before I set a foot down.

So focused was I on where I was stepping that I didn't see two men emerge out of the fog until they were nearly alongside us. They carried another bag between them. It swung with each step, sagging with weight. The man in front stumbled on the wet slag, cursing as the bag hit the ground.

He pulled himself erect and when he lifted his end the bag split in the middle and the shoulder and remains of an arm, severed above the elbow, slid out and landed on the siding with a sodden thud. More would have followed, but the man in the rear dropped his end of the bag in horror and the severed arm and the shoulder settled on the gravel like a half-unwrapped birthday present. Tom Lund had waited for the train to hit him dressed in a new blue and gray flannel shirt.

. . .

I HAD BEEN a journalism student. I knew what I was supposed to do. I had to get reaction. I had to call the family. The deputy sheriff radioed Mac, the police chief, who knew their name and where they lived. He said they had been told. I tried to call them from the pay phone outside the café, but the line was busy. I tried three times and then I stood beneath the café's overhang and watched the rain fall.

He had been sad. That was what his daughter had said when Mac told her. Tom Lund had been sad since his wife had gotten sick with cancer a year and a half ago. What was there to say beyond that? What was there to ask? Did I really want to do this? It felt like I had been playing at being a journalist, covering high school sports but nothing that mattered, taking part in some sort of harmless game that had, without warning, become too real. I stood there for a while, cold and wet and uncertain, before I ran through the rain to my car.

The house was in the older part of town, a small white two-story box with concrete steps and an entry that looked like it had been added on. Two-thirds of the houses in the Great Plains look just like that. I couldn't find a doorbell. The curtains were drawn. No one had noticed me on the step. It would be possible, still, to turn around and drive away. I could choose not to do this.

I raised my fist. For a moment it felt as if it met some invisible resistance in the air, and then it came down, surprisingly hard, on the door.

. . .

I WAS WRITING the story when Art and Louise appeared beside my desk. Art was short, slightly plump. Standing there, they made up the classic mismatched comedy duo, short and tall, fat and thin, watery and fire-eyed, the paper's very own Abbott and Costello, united in their concern about the responsibility that had suddenly landed in the hands of their twenty-year-old sports reporter.

"You talked to the Lund family?"

Art was a printer by trade; he loved the intricacy of machines, had a knack with them. People were more difficult. He had a gentle, almost childlike voice, and when he was nervous his speech slowed down, as if he found each word a mild embarrassment. It made him sound even more hesitant than usual, and he was the kind of guy who hesitated at hello.

I nodded. I was trying to hold on to the sentence I was writing.

"You got a picture?" Louise asked. "We need a picture."

I nodded toward the Polaroid sitting on the right side of my typewriter. An old man stood behind a wheelchair occupied by his wife. He had a burr of white hair and a weathered face earned through a life of outdoor work. His arms were rope-thin, his spine as straight as a hammered-in fence post. He was leaning forward and his hands were on the shoulders of his wife, whose body had collapsed into the shape of an aged newborn. She sat crumpled and sideways in the voluminous wheelchair, her sunken, birdlike face averted from the camera.

"It's the last one they have of him." I saw the horror in both their eyes; obituaries were supposed to be a fresh linen draped over a life, not a police Polaroid that allowed you to see all the wounds.

"I also got this." I slid the photo over to uncover a younger Thomas Lund sitting in a fishing boat along a dock, an uncomplicated smile on his face.

Art nodded with relief, but Louise was considering me with interest.

"You like the first one, Ricky?"

"I think so . . . yeah."

"Why?"

It was a fair question. Why did I want people to see this?

"He sat down on the railroad tracks and let himself get run over by a coal train. He did it after spending three hours with his wife. Theresa, her name is Theresa. She's dying of pancratic cancer. They were married forty-eight years ago last week . . ."

I looked at the paper in my typewriter. I had a page and a half written and another page or so to go. The piece wasn't going to be long, but I knew it was the first meaningful thing I had written in my life, and I wanted to get it right. I wanted it to come together. I wasn't going to tie everything up neatly, as if one thing explained the next, but if I could just lay it out properly—the anniversary celebration at the hospital, the new drugs for her pain that weren't working, the hours by her side, the unmade bed in the attic room where Thomas Lund was staying with his daughter, and then the tracks, the rain, the fog, the fact no one had noticed him, not even the train's engineers, until it was too late—if I could just work through this in the right order and say it properly, I thought there might be understanding and, if nothing else, at least the small dignity of having your story told for Thomas Lund, whom I had never heard of before this day.

"I just think it's part of the story."

Art rubbed his nervous hands together and looked at Louise, whose fiery eye was burning a hole through my forehead. She nodded and smiled.

"You're the editor, Ricky . . . *Wheee.*"

They disappeared out the front door together. Maybe, I thought. For now. All I really knew was how much I wanted to finish the story and get it right. I was lost in the words on the page again when I felt a presence at my shoulder.

"Pan-*creat*-ic," Anna said, so only I could hear. "Not pan-*crat*-ic. Pancreatic cancer."

Chapter 4

SO OFTEN WE DON'T SEE THE THINGS that matter to the people who matter to us until too late. Anna had two children, a twelve-year-old boy and a younger girl, beautiful children I never paid any real attention to at the time. They lived on the frayed edge of Shannon on a street that ended on a bluff above a weed-choked ravine usually festooned with yellowing newspapers and other stray garbage. The Farmers Home Administration was, then, the federal agency that provided low-interest home loans to qualified—meaning poor—rural Americans. FmHA houses had a sameness about them, small ranch homes without adornment or grace. They were approved and built individually, but clustered, for some reason having to do with real estate values, in certain parts of town.

In Shannon they were on the north side of town, which was the direction of the prevailing wind and had a wild, Scottish moors feel about it. In winter the snow piled up shoulder-high against exposed walls. In the summer the dust blew in unimpeded for two hundred miles and the leaves on the trees had a gritty sheen.

I drove up there many times, several because Anna's old Buick was always breaking down and she needed a ride (I would never have known if Christina, a waitress at the café and Anna's friend, hadn't told me about her car problems one day during lunch) and once because of the only party Anna ever threw—but that comes later.

What always struck me when I drove up was how desolate it was and how the homes felt more connected to the country than the town. At some point I learned Anna was from out there, the far western reaches of the state, where the land grows even more empty and harsh, the badlands with their bare-assed buttes and seamed-and-cracked terrain like some unpopulated backwater of the Greek underworld.

The windows in her kitchen, where I imagine her starting every day, looked backward toward her past, with nothing in between her and the place she had fled. I think about that now, and I admire, more than I had sense to at the time, how she walked out of her house with the quiet, chin-up determination I still remember, all these years later.

She didn't have enough money, of course. None of us did. The newspaper came close to paying us with grocery coupons. But there wasn't much to spend money on in Shannon, anyway. The best thing about the small, perpetually dying towns dotting the forgotten middle of the nation might be that it's still possible to be poor in them with some dignity. Not that any of that registered at the time. I'd dropped out of school, was living in an abandoned dentist's office without a fridge, driving a five-year-old Camaro, had barely enough spare change for pizza and beer, and was trying to believe, with the anxious and arrogant blindness of youth, that it signaled absolutely nothing about my future prospects.

And here was this woman, raising two children on no more than I was making. It had to be a life where every dime counted, where every choice had to be measured, and I never gave it the thought I should have. But then, there were a lot of things I should have paid more attention to that year.

. . .

THE FIRST TIME I picked Anna up at her home we drove past a little girl on a tricycle circling the concrete slab for a house that had never been built. She was wearing a stained pink jacket and a knit stocking cap, even though it was spring, and her long, pale hair flew sideways. There seemed to be no one watching over her.

"What does your family do, Eric?" Anna asked, staring out the window at the girl accelerating in an ever-tightening spiral.

"My parents are teachers. University professors. And yours, what do they do?"

"They pretend to ranch."

"Ah," I said because I decided it was some kind of joke. "Unicorns."

"Something like that."

We drove on down the hill and had nearly reached Main Street when Anna said, "We need to go back."

"You forgot something?"

"The little girl. We need to go back. There was no one around, and I've never seen her before. We need to go back."

I looked at her and, for the first time, it really registered how pretty she was. Very, *very* old to a twenty-year-old, of course, quite possibly older than thirty, and with children—odd little creatures she had given birth to with, I imagined, some western-cowboy-type-guy in the distant past—but definitely pretty, maybe even beautiful, oval face, dark, liquid eyes framed by the twin arches of heavy but not oppressive brows. She was slim and small, but not too small, not one of those china-doll women, not fragile, but self-contained and somehow sturdy, despite her size. Her hair was a lustrous mahogany that went coal-black in the sun and her skin had a faintly olive tone, a shadow of Mediterranean color that marked her off from the vanilla-skinned Scandinavians that clogged the local gene pool. Her eyes were the thing you noticed, but her lips were also unusually dark, the color of spilled wine.

Still, she was *much* older, and my coworker, and I had an overly developed sense of propriety about these things, so I put her lips and all the rest out of my mind.

We drove back up the hill and the little girl was gone. Anna stood on the abandoned concrete slab and turned slowly in a circle, as if she might spot her in the distance.

"I'm sure it's fine," I said. "She just went home."

"I never saw her before. My kids play with the other kids."

"She's probably just visiting."

"I don't think so."

"Then they're new."

"Maybe."

I had a chamber of commerce story to write and I wanted to get to the office, but there was something about the way Anna stood there on that godforsaken abandoned slab.

"We can knock on some doors, if you want."

It was cold. She had her arms crossed, hugging herself, and I noticed the sleeves of her blouse were too long; she held the end of each one in place in the palm of her hand so they didn't slide back.

"It's okay," she said, as if we had failed somehow. "We tried."

Now I felt stubborn.

"No, we can check. We're *reporters*."

Anna smiled the distant and quietly sad smile I would come to know so well, the one that felt as if she weren't smiling at you, but at some slightly awkward joke she remembered from long ago.

"People don't care that much, Eric. Not really. It's unicorn ranching. And I have retired. It was just silly. I'm sure she's fine."

She led the way back to the car, and so much of everything I needed to understand about her was right there.

• • •

I WAS YOUNG. This will be my reoccurring excuse, and here I offer an additional defense: my thoughts, at the time, were elsewhere. I had agreed to take over a small newspaper, without any real idea what that meant.

What it meant was several things, but small newspapers, first and foremost, are about gossip. The social notes, a record of the most mundane small-town comings and goings—*Mildred Olson visited Loraine Lillehaugen Sunday at the Shady Acres Home for the Retired . . . The regular meeting of the Busy Bees Quilting Society met at Colleen Polka's Tuesday*—were handled by Edith Swenson, a tall, older woman with iron-gray hair and fiercely square shoulders, who showed up on Tuesdays, a couple of days before we went to press, and sorted through the handwritten scraps of paper that had been dropped off at the front desk. Edith had lived in Shannon since the days of wild bison wandering the prairie and seemed to know much of the social news in advance, as if by osmosis. Most importantly, she knew the correct spelling of every single family name in the county.

Next to *The Family Circus*, the social notes were the most popular thing in the paper and filled up one of the back pages. The front page and the jump page were the editor's—now my—responsibility. Sports generally had one page. That left the middle pages, largely filled with the routine events—rotary club meetings, fund-raising breakfasts, high school award winners—that small-town papers pretend are news. Depending on my desperation, any of these items could be elevated to the front, but in general they filled up the inside.

Those were Anna's pages and she tended to them as she had before I took over, writing short, simple, straightforward stories. To be honest, at first I don't think it really occurred to me that she worked for me. Later, I would get her to write longer features about local events and oddball characters, always a plentiful resource in backwater towns, and the unaffected nature of her prose would come through. She wrote clearly and precisely, and these are no small things. I wish now I had told her that more forcefully. She was invisible inside her own stories, so no one paid them much mind, but they were good. She had an unclouded eye. Nobody gives a shit anymore in America about the people quietly paying attention, but that was Anna.

Of course, part of the reason nobody noticed might have been that so much of what we did was so mind-numbingly boring that paying close attention was akin to sensory deprivation. Chronicling life in Shannon was a lot like waiting for the seasons to change in Antarctica. The penguins might notice it's warmer, but, really, it's cold, it's white, and that glacier off to the north looks pretty much the way it has for the last ten thousand years.

So Anna did her work and in the beginning I left her to it, not even sure what it amounted to. We sat five feet apart and did our separate things. The exception was Thursday nights, when we laid out the paper together.

. . .

THE DAY STARTED with the paper as busy as it ever was—Anna, Edith, and I finishing up our copy in the morning, the part-time typesetters working furiously in the afternoon while I printed the final photos in the darkroom, Todd and Paul hurrying to get other press runs out of the way while Art and Louise fretted about, then Anna and I working on the layout at the glass-topped light tables in the back.

There came a time, after dinner, when we were usually alone. Either Todd or Paul would come back to run the presses when we were finished, but until then, it was just the two of us laying out the pages, running strips of copy through the waxing machine and placing them on the empty broadsheets with their faint blue lines illuminated by the tables.

The back shop was industrial: high I-beamed ceiling, concrete floors, the skeletal frame of the main printing press hovering in the shadows like the desiccated remains of a dinosaur. Odd pieces of machinery were scattered about, including an old hand-set letterpress with a giant metal wheel straight out of Dickens that Art still loved to use whenever he could find an excuse. We had a radio we tuned to the local station, which played a mix of sixties rock and forlorn country, but we kept it low. The lights, too, were turned down so we could see the blue lines shining through the pages.

The atmosphere was gloomy and intimate, a cross between an abandoned factory and a gone-to-seed museum. The work was exacting—you needed to make sure everything was in the right place and perfectly straight—but also restful, like working on a familiar jigsaw puzzle. It took one part of your attention, but not another. So we talked. We had hours and we talked. We had many Thursday nights over many weeks and months, and we talked.

Okay, mostly I talked. I was twenty and quite pleased with the depth and dimension of my own thoughts—thoughts on politics, history, sports, literature, movies, television, how to solve global hunger, end war, time travel, raise children, and discipline pets.

"Vietnam was the end," I remember saying one of our first nights together. A story about the war, which was not so far past then, had been in the news. "There'll never be another war. Not for the United States."

Anna's eyes remained focused on her page.

"You think so?"

"Sure, we got our butts kicked. We're not going to make that mistake again. Besides, who else is there to fight, really? The Russians? That would be the end of everything."

"People find a reason to fight."

"It's not going to happen. The only wars left are little wars, and we've learned our lesson." I could see all of human history laid out in front of me as clearly as the columns on my layout sheet. America had turned a page. We would have no more wars.

"We've learned," I said. "No more wars."

"Well, then. That's good. I've been waiting for the moment when human nature changes."

The woman in partial silhouette beside me seemed to be smiling ever so slightly; it could simply have been with satisfaction at the page she had finished and was sliding to the side.

"Oh, okay," I said. "But I really think we're done. History marches on."

She was searching for her X-Acto knife, which I had picked up. When I handed it back to her I could see her half-hidden amusement.

"It does," I insisted.

"Really?"

"Yes. You don't think so?"

Anna carefully took the knife from my hand.

"I would say history hangs around, Eric."

Not only did I seem to be losing an argument, when I

knew I was right, but she was somehow getting twice as much work done as I was. It was all annoying. I focused on my own half-finished page, which made the rest of the room recede into shadow.

"Yes, okay. Humans are humans. *Sure*. But there's progress. Look at medicine. CAT scans. Heart transplants. You can't say things haven't changed."

"You can't."

I saw I had forgotten to put a border around the photograph. I searched the edges of the table for the tape.

"That's right," I said. "Progress."

"Progress."

"*Progress*. Someday we'll look back at this era of medicine and it'll seem closer to bloodletting with leaches than real science."

Anna handed me the border tape.

"Someday?"

Now I knew I was being teased.

"Yes, because science—"

"Marches on?"

"Yes!"

I pointed to the old cast-iron letterpress, with its gigantic hand wheel, and the shining steel bus-sized modern press with its hundred electric motors behind us. "You can't say science—technology—doesn't march on."

"You sure can't."

"There!"

I stepped back in triumph to consider my page, which I thought was also now successfully concluded, until I realized the bottom of the picture still needed to be trimmed. I looked around for the scissors.

Anna retrieved them from behind the coffeepot, where I had left them just minutes earlier.

"But maybe *people* move a little more in circles."

Many years later I was writing a story on the gap between academic achievement and self-regard—a study had found that the less students knew, the more likely they were to rate their level of knowledge highly—and the expert I was interviewing observed, "You have to know something before you can see how much you really have to learn." The satisfied sound of my voice, as hollow as the sound from a pennywhistle, echoes back across the years, and I cringe a little.

But at that moment, standing with my hand outstretched for the scissors, our eyes met. I expected to see triumph or even mockery, but I still remember how Anna's held a bemused delight, as if I'd brought something new and unexpected into the day, even if I was clearly, hopelessly wrong.

And suddenly I was laughing at myself, which is never a bad thing for a twenty-year-old.

Chapter 5

WAS IT THE NEXT THURSDAY, or was it a week or two later, when she began to tell me about her past? I don't know. Those early nights in the back shop, moving in and out of the Gothic shadows, moving in out of the rectangles of blue light, float in my memory like one long night. Hours and hours of the two of us together, talking. The Anna dialogues.

She had that cigarette-stained voice and she almost always spoke softly, so much so she was hard to hear if she was looking down, focused on her work. Yet there was also a precision to her cadence, a clarity. She didn't speak slowly; she spoke carefully, as if each word had been given an extra moment to set in some clear, clean space in Anna's head, just to see how it stood up. This was true except in those moments when an odd thing I had said made her laugh, or caught her fancy in some other way, and then she could respond in a slightly breathless rush, her words rising at the end of sentences so she sounded unexpectedly girlish. Unexpected to a twenty-year-old. She was really not so old, after all.

I spend so much time on Anna's voice because it remains so alive in my memory, woven in and out of the half darkness and the tin sound of the radio turned low in that quiet, echoing room.

On this night, we had been talking about the possibility of life on other planets. A Mars lander some years earlier had done tests that had yielded mixed signals. I wanted to believe, but Anna was quietly dubious.

"Maybe," she said. "But I think we would know."

Maybe was a word with multiple lives when spoken by Anna. It could stand as a kindhearted policeman, signaling disagreement or correction, but it could also take the bench as a magistrate, reserving judgment until all the facts were in, or as the keeper of the keys, guarding the private rooms of other lives. This *maybe* was a polite no, which annoyed me.

"How would we know?" I said. "It's on other *planets*."

"Yes," Anna said, which was really a slightly firmer no.

"Come on . . . Other planets! *Mars*. Far away. Little dot. Used to think it had canals, *Martians*, little green guys with death rays."

Her eyes remained fastened on her light table, but she smiled.

"Oh, if they'd found little green guys with death rays, I'd believe that."

"But not bacteria or, like, single-cell organisms?"

"Nope."

"All right."

"If life was there, I just don't think we'd have to hunt for it so hard," Anna said. "I think it would be more than a few bacteria in the soil. If life exists, it finds a way."

I realized, with a mild feeling of discouragement, that this made too much sense for a blithe retort. "Riders on the Storm" by the Doors came on the radio, the wash of rain and thunder that opens the song sounding oddly real through the cheap speaker.

"I didn't know you were a biologist," I said finally, trying to sound sarcastic but more or less nailing peevish.

Anna laughed. "I'm a naturalist of all sorts. I grew up surrounded by nothing but plant life and cows."

"I thought there were unicorns."

She turned to look at me, smiling but confused.

"Unicorn ranching. You brought it up one day when I picked you up."

"Oh, yes. Well, they were free-range. They hardly ever came by the house."

I was working on something clever to say when Anna said, "I love this song. I used to love it when it came on the radio. At night. I loved it. I loved it best when it was really raining, or if there was lightning on the horizon. I loved the way the world and the song melted together."

Those words, coming in a tumble, cracked open the door into her past. I could see a girl lying in bed, listening to that song, a flash of lightning across the flat western sky, and I was curious, intensely curious, about that girl who had somehow turned into this woman who had a weird gift for keeping me off balance.

"It was a quiet life," Anna said, half embarrassed.

"But you grew up on a ranch?"

"Sort of."

"Sort of?"

"A *ranch* might be an exaggeration, Eric. It was a kind of a small farm."

"But out West, the western part of the state, the badlands—" I waved my hand to indicate someplace very far away and distant.

Anna was leaning against her light table now, her arms crossed across her chest. She shook her head in a combination of exasperation and amusement.

"On the edge of the badlands, yes. There were rumors of little green men with death rays."

"No, seriously. What was it like?"

She turned back to the page on her table, staring down into the light, hesitant, but pleased also, I thought, to be asked.

"It was quiet . . ." Anna said again, and that was the start. Over many nights, in fragments, she told me her story. The effect was like turning something broken over in your hand and trying to imagine it whole. Still, across those hours, bent over our boxed-up miniature suns, carefully placing the words we had written on the glowing paper, the girl listening to the radio in her bedroom came to life. If I found out later she had left things out, if I came to see how the things we leave out are often the painfully unsorted heart of the story, I would forgive her for that because I was somehow aware, from the beginning, of the trust she was placing in me.

Chapter 6

SHE REMEMBERED HER CHILDHOOD HOME as empty. Her father always out working. Her mother present but silent, busy with household tasks she attended to without asking for or needing help. They were not unhappy, her parents. She never had a sense they were unhappy but for the wearying, never-ending desperation of not having enough money, of having to weigh every single expenditure of every single cent as if it included some vast and incalculable moral judgment. *I do this and tomorrow I shall be found wanting and I will have failed those I love.* They were not unhappy with who they were, or even with what they had most of the time, but they were tired and it had rendered them timid and sad in some less essential, but still all-encompassing way.

The problem was simply that they didn't have enough land. In western North Dakota you need a lot of land before you have enough land for it to mean anything. There was oil in the area and later some families got very rich, but Anna's family was forever in the wrong spot when it came to good fortune.

She was their only child and they seemed not to know quite what to do with her. She came late and their habits had all been established. They were not the type to ask for help and it didn't occur to them that asking their own daughter to pitch in was different. Still, she inherited their dutifulness and tried to make herself useful. A set of chores eventually evolved that she tended to, helping her mother deal with the unending dust and mud, feeding the dog and pretending to feed the cats, who actually lived on mice in the lean-to shed they called a barn. They had a windmill that turned the pump that filled the water trough near the barn, but the gears stuck, and by the time she was twelve, she was the member of the family who climbed the rusting metal frame to tug the chain back into motion.

It was her favorite chore, balanced high in the air, holding on with one hand while she leaned back into the wind to reach the gears. Her hair blew in her eyes and the wild, empty country tilted around her and she could see forever. The autumnal prairie and the light caught in the tangle of her hair were the same golden color and she both floated above and felt part of the land as the pump chugged back to life. I can picture her there, a skinny, beautiful girl, a fiercely carved figure on the prow of a ship, ready to set sail.

She had hours on her own. They lived too far from town for her to go in casually, even later when she was a teenager. During the school year the bus arrived at the end of their long and badly kept farm road, took her off, and brought her back eight hours later. But that left endless time, time as deep and shadowed as a German forest, time for her mind to go anywhere. At school they visited the public library every Friday afternoon and so she always had books and, at home, plenty of time to read. There was nothing much else to do. She read and, although she never told me this, never boasted once that I can remember, I am sure got excellent grades at school and sat bored and dreaming in the back of the classroom half the time. The Great Plains make dreamers the way New York makes hustlers, and Anna was another one of them, another quiet girl in the back of the class in a faded dress with her mind a thousand miles from the only place she knew.

The badlands in western North Dakota are striped with veins of lignite, which are sometimes ignited by lightning. They can burn for weeks, months, or even years, and that was Anna's first memory: a line of fire on the rim of the night sky visible from her bedroom window. The fires came and went when she was a child, but by the time she was thirteen one had come to haunt her. She lay in bed and the bent and narrow flame floating just below the stars was an umbilical cord pulling her toward some spark of life. She watched the colors shift, assume harlequin forms in the narrow furnace, and she was filled with a longing as elusive as the figures that rose and dissolved in the flames.

Of course, it was only a matter of time until she met a boy.

. . .

HE WORKED ON AN OIL RIG. He was from somewhere else. He had a shock of blond hair like a flare of sun and a face that was all perfect angles smudged with the greasy war paint of his adventure. He wore Levi's that were a little too tight and T-shirts that were a little too large and his black Pontiac Firebird flew across the hills trailing a plume of dust that rose into the prairie sunset.

I never heard his name. In all those hours we spent together she never said it. In fact, she almost never referred to him directly. He was the figure in the story whose outline you could only trace by the way the others moved around his unseen presence. So here the story departs from Anna's own hesitant, fractured narration. Here the story is picked up by Christina, the waitress at the café whom Anna had confided in at some desolate moment in the past, and who told me all she knew one night after too many drinks in the Buffalo Bar.

Anna was sixteen. She had been to a dance at the high school and had asked the friend who was driving her home to drop her off at the turn a mile from her house. Her heart was overfull with music and dancing and the confused longing in the eyes of the boys who stood on the far side of the gym working up their courage. She wanted to walk to settle her thoughts. It never occurred to her to worry about being alone in the country. This was her home and it was empty but for the brilliant stars and the shadows of the hills and the moon already distant on the far side of the sky.

She saw the car coming from a long ways away. No one came down this road but her own family and the old couple that lived another five miles farther west, and they never drove this fast. She stood on the shoulder of the asphalt, watching the car race toward her, and at the last moment she realized she was too close, she should step down into the ditch, make herself safe and invisible, but the car was already upon her, headlights on bright, a tunnel of light that swallowed Anna, tore her soul briefly loose from her body, and then passed, leaving her windswept, tasting dust, staring dazed at receding red taillights.

The car braked to a sliding stop and made a precise three-point turn. The window rolled down and she saw the silhouette of a man or a boy.

"You lost?" The voice was still indeterminate, although it had a lilt. Southern.

"No."

"Good. Because I am. I'm trying to get to Haversford."

"You haven't come to the turn. It's about half a mile up."

"Cool."

A boy.

"You go right. It's about five miles."

He leaned forward and the dashboard filled the startling hollows of his face with green light.

"That's great. Thank you."

"Okay."

She started to walk and saw the car was trailing along beside her.

"I heard there's a dance there tonight."

"There was. A high school dance."

"High school? Shit."

"It's over now."

She was walking a little faster, but the car matched her pace.

"Yeah? Well . . . you want to come into town anyway?"

"No. Thank you."

"Why not?"

"I have to get home."

He moved slightly and the green light lit a corner of his smile.

"You're in the middle of nowhere."

"My home's right up the road here."

"No kidding? Well . . . I'll bring you right back."

"No, thanks."

"Come on. I'll buy you a Coke or something."

"No. Everything's closed." She was walking as fast as she could now without running and felt slightly out of breath.

"No shit? Well, just a drive. You can show me the sights."

"There are no sights."

"Is there a streetlight?"

She stopped. "What?"

"A streetlight. You know, like a lamp hanging from a pole."

She had to think about this.

"Yes. On Main Street."

"What's your name?"

"My name?"

"Yes, your name. What's your name?"

"Anna."

"All right. Anna, I would like to see that streetlight. I haven't seen a single streetlight since I came up here. I would like to see that streetlight with you."

He leaned across the seat and opened the passenger door. The dome light came on and she got her first good look at him.

"About a half a mile up," she said, "on your right, you can't miss it." And she was running, stumbling down into the ditch and across the broken pasture toward the lights of her home, and she was never sure because of the roar in her head from her own ragged breathing, but she thought she heard him laughing.

Lying in bed that night, wide awake, watching the hills smolder, unable to stand the weight of the covers pressing against her, she kicked them aside and felt a warmth, a mild electric current working itself up her body. She saw the hard planes of his arms and shoulders etched in the shadows, the way his face with its hollow cheeks, thin, serious mouth, and glinting eyes emerged in the light, and she thought, *He knows where I live.*

Of course, I can't know that last part. The story Christina told me ends with Anna running through the dark toward her home. But there was always a longing about Anna, a wistfulness for some lost thing that surfaced at odd times. She would hesitate over the perfect egg of a stone left behind on a lakeshore, the pattern of a cobweb in a window, a pinwheel of light through a rotting barn wall. Yes, these are moments of stray beauty that can capture anyone, but they seemed like something more to her. She would pick up the stone, brush the cobweb, hesitate in the pins of light, and there was a sadness when she set them aside, as if some elusive connection had been missed.

So I see her in bed that night, and whether the hills were burning or not, whether it was hot or cold in her room, whether she kicked the covers aside or pulled them closer, I know her thoughts, and they were that she had been found.

Chapter 7

WE WERE BECOMING FRIENDS, good friends, I thought, and yet there were mysteries, always, things I could not fit into the woman I was coming to know. They were there from the beginning. Like sudden changes in the weather.

"Okay," I said to Todd, "I'll buy one."

"That's funny."

"I'm serious. I'll buy one."

"No, man, it was just *practice*."

"I know, but I need a vacuum. I really do. My apartment has carpet."

The thatch of straw on the top of Todd's head seemed to stand up even straighter in alarm.

"No. But. Man. It costs *five hundred* dollars!"

"But there's an installment plan. You said so yourself."

"Jesus, Ricky. I didn't—"

"You're trying to sell vacuum cleaners, right? Well, I'm buying one."

A late spring storm had blown in, a blizzard that had trapped us all, knocking out the electricity in my building and forcing me to move in with Todd, who rented a small house from the Shoemakers directly across from the newspaper office. We'd been thrown together for three days and, among many things, I'd discovered that Todd had been driving to Bismarck on weekends and training to become a door-to-door vacuum cleaner salesman. The last step in the training was a full dress rehearsal sales pitch in front of a friend. With no one going anywhere, I had qualified.

He stared at the shining metal machine at his feet: the best vacuum cleaner known to man—or so he had just spent the last half hour telling me.

"I can't do this. I can't sell these things."

"Do you really need the money?"

"I don't know. I just thought it would be something to do."

"You can't feel guilt as a salesman."

"I don't feel *guilt*, man. I just don't like ripping people off."

"Okay. Still, it could be a problem."

"Yeah . . . You shouldn't buy one. Five hundred bucks, that's crazy."

"I do need a vacuum cleaner. I should clean my place every once in a while."

"You can borrow my old Hoover, man. It works fine."

"All right."

"Cool."

Todd kicked the vacuum cleaner over with the ball of his foot. We stared out the living room window, the storm an unchanging wall of white painted on the glass. After three days we had stopped hearing the wind except when it seemed to move the old house.

"I think it's getting better out there," Todd said.

I had learned he was a good guy who liked to drink beer and watch wrestling and old *Andy Griffith* reruns. He was willing to watch almost anything, however, and we'd survived seventy-two hours together on Budweiser and cable. But the Budweiser was almost gone, and after last night's horror movie marathon, so was the cable.

"It's definitely getting better," I said.

"Definitely."

Slumped on the couch, Todd stared into his can of beer and squished it. The Wile E. Coyote tattoo on his bicep scrunched up as if Wile E. had just been hit by an anvil.

"You really gonna put out a paper this week?"

"Art says they've never missed an issue."

"What are you going to fill it with?"

"Well, there's a storm."

Todd smiled. "I guess that's news. I'll be running the presses. Paul's buried alive out there."

"Cool."

"Yeah."

"Yeah."

"Yeah."

He slumped on the couch while I remained sunk in the overstuffed chair he had picked up at some rummage sale. The remote control lay on the floor, tragically just out of the reach of both of us.

"I'll call the city office and find out when we'll get dug out," I said, just to say something. "I'll take some pictures downtown, and I'll get Anna to take some up her way."

Todd grimaced.

"What? There's something else?"

"No, no, man, it's nothing like that. It's just . . . Anna doesn't do so good in storms."

I didn't think I'd heard him right. "Do so good in storms?"

"Yeah. Snowstorms. She doesn't function so well in them . . . Well, doesn't function at all in them, really."

He tossed his empty beer can toward the trash can. Wile E. Coyote jumped as if stuck by a pitchfork.

"Wait a minute. She lives in North Dakota—she was *born* in North Dakota—and she doesn't do so well in *snow*storms?"

He shrugged. "You remember the big storm we had last year? No, you weren't here yet. We had this big storm, probably bigger than this one, and it knocked everything down, and Stacy—she was our editor then—was stuck out of town, so Art and Louise had to take over, and they were trying to get Anna to help, and she wouldn't answer her phone. They called her every couple of hours and you could hear it ringing on the other end of the line, and where could she be, right? But she wouldn't pick up. Not just during the storm, but a couple of days afterward, too, when it was just clear and cold, and everybody was trying to dig out and get things started up again. So Art's getting worried, and he sends me up there. Paul has a snowmobile. I took that. It was a blast, man. There were snowbanks so high I was driving past people's second-story windows."

"Where was she?"

His grin dissolved into a look of confusion.

"She was home. It wasn't even so bad up there. The wind had blown most of the snow down into the valley. The ridges were really pretty bare. There were a bunch of kids out playing in that gulch they got up there, digging tunnels and building forts. I look, but I can't see her kids. I knock and I stand in the doorway for a while and then I get worried. I mean, it just didn't seem right, you know, so I try the door and it's not locked and I open it and step into the kitchen and I call her."

He hesitated, probably wishing he hadn't started this story.

"So her boy, the older one, comes running out of the back of the house. He looks scared until he recognizes me. The little girl just peeks around the corner. I ask them if their mom's okay, and they both nod, but, you know, it just feels weird. I'm standing there, trying to figure out what to do, and Anna comes around the corner. She's wearing a robe and it looks like she hasn't been out of bed or taken a shower, man, for a week."

He paused again, even more uncomfortable.

"You want a beer?" I said.

He nodded gratefully. When I came back from the kitchen he opened his beer and took a drink.

"So I ask Anna if she's sick, and she kind of shakes her head, like she doesn't understand the question or something. The kids are looking worried, and I wonder why they're not out there with all the other kids. Snow day, right? And I'm wondering what I should do, call Art or the police or something. And Anna says, 'It's bad weather. It's just bad weather. Tell Art I'm sorry. I'll be in tomorrow.'"

Todd shrugged and took a drink of beer. In the kitchen the back door shuddered once in the wind.

"Have you ever noticed," I said, "that she always wears sleeves that are too long?"

"Yeah, that's weird, too."

"What do you think was going on?"

He looked down at his bicep and flexed. He was a skinny guy and it really wasn't that impressive.

"I don't know, man, I'm just the printer. I think she doesn't do so well in snowstorms."

That was already many years after she met the boy, where Anna's winter begins, and it was months before I would finally hear the story. But when I remember Todd telling me this, I see Anna out in a storm, stumbling down the steps and into a blind world where everything disappears and, far too late for it to matter, I understand.

Chapter 8

I SAID MY PARENTS WERE COLLEGE TEACHERS, but what I didn't tell you was that my father wasn't teaching anymore when I dropped out of school. He'd had the first of the strokes that would eventually kill him, and he was stuck at home, half blind, an erratic parody of the man he had been, some parts of his personality larger, some smaller, some strangely shaded, a familiar portrait with the colors all slightly off. My mother was still teaching and trying to hold everything together, including keeping track of my younger brother and sister, both in high school and trouble, roughly to the same degree.

I came home right after the stroke, stood at the side of the hospital bed, and listened to my father, a brilliant man, loop through a two-minute conversation repeated over and over as the beginning disappeared from his mind before he reached the end. We had always been close in the way of fathers and sons who can't get along because they are bound by the same flaws, and seeing him there with part of his mind sheared away was like being severed from my own connection to the material world. The doctors would get him on blood thinners and God knows what other meds and his memory would get better, but not so many other things.

I went back to the university and missed most of the worst, but college life, which already echoed with too much of my young past, now felt as insignificant as a children's play put on in the basement on a slow winter day. There was no real reason why I was there. I'd gone to school and taken up journalism because I liked reading, I didn't mind writing, and there seemed to be very little math. I also liked that it wasn't teaching; my parents' life had left me with a dread of the desiccated, chalk-filled routines of the classroom. But my choices were no more profound than that; they were a stall, a delay. Somewhere up ahead, I was sure, my life would take up its main course and become a raging Amazon of purpose and direction, even if it had so far been a series of meandering, minor eddies in which I drifted along until the course ran dry.

Now, with my father's illness, what had been the best thing about going to school, the sense of stealing time from responsibility, was barren, attended by a constant whisper of shame. Everyone said I should stay in school and I knew I should be at home helping out. The problem was I couldn't make myself believe I would be any real help at all.

What you want desperately at a time like that is for something to mean something to you, not the thing you are fleeing, but something else. I had been seeing Emily since shortly after arriving at the university, when I first stumbled into her sneaking into the bathroom in my dorm one morning. It was a men's dorm and she'd spent the night with someone—I was smart enough never to ask who—and she was wearing an oversized Clash T-shirt and nothing else, which was really all it took. I complimented her on the shirt, stepped back out the door, and waited until she was finished. But when I left the bathroom, she was waiting in the hall and asked if I wanted to get a coffee. I said it seemed she might be busy; she said that had been a mistake and was over. She might have been discussing some half-forgotten annoyance that had happened in the distant past, perhaps another life completely.

"Give me five minutes," she said, running down the hall, stopping, and turning once to consider me. "You know, you look a little like Mick Jones."

I don't really, not at all. But we liked the same music and we liked playing tennis and getting late-night Mexican. If we were ill suited in other ways more profound and complicated than either of us wanted to think about, well, it was college and there were certainly stranger couples than we were.

Still, there were times when I was walking across the campus at night to meet up with Emily and each step seemed to get heavier and heavier until I stopped and leaned against a wall with a leaden sense of defeat. She was pretty, sexy in a slightly old-fashioned way, bobbed blond hair, startling light blue eyes, and a sensual mouth, and, if I'm honest, that was why I always kept walking. The truth is, we were a fallback couple pretending to each other we were something more, spending time with our arms draped around each other at parties while measuring other possibilities out of the corners of our eyes.

This was how it was, anyway, until shortly before my

father's stroke, when Emily started seeing the owner of a club everyone went to. He was young for a businessman, but a lot older than those of us who were making him prematurely wealthy. Suddenly I had lost my girl, if I'd ever really been able to call her that, and the place I went to most often at night. How I might have measured the relative weight of these losses I can't tell you, but on a night after my father had his stroke, I was sitting on the steps of my dorm, staring across the campus quad. The quad had a flagpole at its center where all the sidewalks met like the spokes of a wheel. Emily and a girl I didn't know appeared out of the shadows beside the Student Union and started across, moving in and out of the light from the faux-British streetlamps above the sidewalk.

The night was a stage and, as she stepped from spotlight to spotlight, I found myself waiting for each reappearance with a surprising urgency. I knew her walk. I knew that tilt of her head. I knew the way she held her shoulders and I knew that slightly distracted smile, and the fact I had lost her, had half wanted to lose her, filled me with such panic I couldn't breathe. I had found the thing I wanted, I needed, I had to have, and it made no sense, and I felt it all the more strongly for that. It was all I could do not to run across the grass and tackle her, carrying her away to a cabin in the Rockies or an island in the middle of the Pacific, and yet at the same time, I was aware of the incongruity of my feelings, and that only made it worse, as if I had lost the ability to hold the world in its correct form, had woken up to find some essential part of myself missing.

Not calling her the next two days was like willing myself

not to place my hand over a bleeding wound. The act of *not* acting consumed the totality of my being every minute of each day. I read from my roommate's collection of Louis L'Amour westerns by a lamp until dawn and then closed my eyes briefly before stumbling through classes. The end of my academic career came the following morning in transformational grammar as I stared at the second page of my exam without picking up my pencil for ten minutes, folded the paper so the blank pages weren't visible, brought it to the teacher's desk, pretended I didn't notice his look of concern, walked out of the classroom, down the hall, and out into a day that seemed to explode with color.

I tore the *Sentinel*'s phone number off the bottom of the advertisement and within a week I had my apartment over the bank, was working as a sportswriter, and had left everything and most everyone I knew behind, without bothering to tell anyone at school. And it was only in this sudden, impulsive move from east to west, from the leafy college town on the edge of Minnesota's lake country to the windblown, brown Dakota plains that I felt my sense of self return.

The nights were still long, but the days had a simplicity and order. I had these things to do, and when they were done, I had done the things I had to do, and I could play pool at the Buffalo Bar and eat chicken pot pies late at night and read Travis McGee mysteries and listen to Minnesota Twins games on the radio, and, even before I became the editor, life started to feel okay and then pretty good. It was only at unexpected moments, when my mind had wandered too far into some unmarked cul de sac, that I found myself seeing her short, tousled blond hair and wide, crooked smile that still did something to me, slightly blurred my vision. But it wasn't that often and most of the time I felt pretty good.

Really, it was entirely possible I felt fine.

You don't need anyone else that badly. You can live just fine by attending to the day in front of you. These were lessons I had learned. These were ideas I had fixed against the chaos. These were the beliefs I held fast on the nights I sat in my blue chair and watched dawn peel away the darkness above Main Street. Yes, I was doing well. I did not need anyone.

Chapter 9

THE THING ABOUT LATE SPRING BLIZZARDS is they're followed by late spring floods. The snow stopped, the sun came out, the sky and earth were the same startling unblemished white, as if God had created the universe ten seconds ago, and then it started to melt, and soon the streets were black and running with dirty water and mud was everywhere and the river was rising too fast.

During my few months in town, the Derry River had been this half-asleep brown snake that wound through the oldest neighborhoods, a quiet presence hidden behind cottonwoods and cedars that you could wade through in spots or skate across in the winter with a single hard push. Now it began creeping up dead lawns, approaching stone foundations already turning black with dampness. The river ran along the edge of downtown and briefly paralleled the railroad tracks, where it was kept back by a low levee that people sometimes sat along on nice days. Soon the water was lapping near the top of the embankment.

Like most every bad thing in life, it was lousy for everybody else, but good for the newspaper business. We had two weeks of real news: storm, melt, rising river, and, best of all, flood. I never saw how Anna did in snowstorms. When the sun came out I spent half a day trudging around town taking pictures, and when I called her the next morning, she was ready to come back to work—paler, perhaps, a little drawn, but businesslike and resolute.

They were piling sandbags along the riverbank by then. Everyone knew what was coming. But an ice dam farther up the river held the water back until it had risen in mass, a sudden lake that came pouring out when the ice gave way, rushing downriver, tearing holes in the dikes and flooding the low-lying parts of town. For a week we worked day and night, taking more pictures, interviewing families forced to leave their homes, the kids and old men and women filling sandbags, the police, the firemen, the mayor.

Art and Louise released everyone else to work on the dikes and then the fallback dikes, so it was just me and Anna putting together the paper. We stumbled in at the end of each day, pants legs covered in mud, hands chapped and raw, heads overfull, to turn what we had learned into news, typing long into the night. It turned out Anna knew how to run every piece of equipment except the press. I handled the darkroom work, watching scenes resolve in the developing tray: houses like floating islands, figures bent over sandbags in the narrow beams of truck lights, men collapsed in exhaustion against the side of their pickups while darts of sleet streaked the picture like static.

Anna did everything else, setting the type and the headlines, designing most of the pages while I typed up the last-minute news. On Thursday night, when we met in the back room to lay out the pages, the building echoed as if we had been forgotten, left behind after the bombs fell. Todd, working now on the reinforced dike being thrown up to keep the water from reaching downtown, was scheduled to show up at midnight to run the presses, but we had no idea exactly what we were going to do with the paper after that, how we were going to get it delivered and who would be there to receive it.

Neither of us had been sleeping much. We had twice as many pages as normal to put together and we were starting late. For the first three hours we worked without saying anything more than necessary. "Have you got the two-point border?" "Can we crop that half an inch?" "We need jump space if we're going to run this full." It was a little after eleven when I straightened up at my light table, feeling the bones in my spine crack back into place, and realized we were going to make it. A rush of exhausted exhilaration swept over me.

"We're going to put out a paper."

Anna smiled tiredly, focused on her work. "That was the idea, yes."

"No, I mean a *paper.* A great paper—in the middle of a flood. A *great* fucking paper, full of all kinds of stuff people want to see. This is what it's all about. This is the whole thing. And we did it!"

I could see she was pleased.

"And you," I said. "You wrote the best thing in here. The story about the Sweeneys losing their home."

This left her flustered. She kept her eyes on the light table.

"Come on. It's good. It's good. It's good!"

Anna shook her head slightly side to side, as if the compliment were a bothersome fly.

"We need to celebrate," I said.

"Maybe we should finish first."

"We're almost finished. We're finished. We can take a five-minute break." I looked around the mausoleum of the back shop in search of our celebration. All I found was the stale coffee in the pot. "We should have brought some beer."

Anna finished laying the last strip of copy into place at the bottom right of a page and stepped back to view it critically.

"Well," she said, "there's Louise's secret stash."

"What?"

"She keeps a bottle in Art's office. You thought she was just naturally like that in the morning?"

. . .

THE HALF-FULL BOTTLE hadn't had a chance to gather any dust. Anna slid it out from behind a stack of *North Dakota Horizons* magazines and twisted open the cap. She poured modest shots into our empty coffee mugs.

"To us." I tipped the mug back.

Anna sipped. "What's so funny?"

"It's blackberry brandy. I drank this when I was a kid . . . What? What's funny about that?"

"Nothing." Anna lifted her mug again. "To the paper."

"*The Shannon Sentinel*, long may she wave."

Art's office was claustrophobic, his grandiose banker's desk piled high with newspapers and other papers teetering on the edge of chaos, the bookshelves lining the walls ready to disgorge a sympathetic landslide of old magazines, notebooks, unopened correspondence, and sheaves of yellowing typewritten pages that probably traced the history of Shannon back to the moment the first railroad surveyor's boots hit the ground. We'd left the lights off, as if we were misbehaving teenagers, so we stood in the middle of this disorder in the pale wedge of light from the half-open door.

It was one of those moments when it's just you and someone else and the rest of the world has vanished, was quite possibly never there to begin with. Yet the stories we had been working on, the photographs we had been staring at, were so alive in my mind they persisted as an afterimage, as if the walls had fallen away and we were simultaneously floating above Shannon and could see the engorged, moonlit river, the men and women behind the dikes, the ordered rows of Monopoly houses waiting for the water, and then, surrounding it all, the vast blank blackness of the state, the eternal frame on our portrait. We were somehow alone and standing close to each other amid all this.

In the suddenly awkward silence Anna's gaze met mine and then slid quickly over my shoulder. I thought she was afflicted with the same double vision: the world, near and far.

"A heck of a storm," I said.

Her already uncertain smile froze.

This bothered me. We had been working together nonstop for hours and I wanted to hold on to the feeling of shared toil and triumph.

"It's been great, hasn't it?" I said.

"Eric."

"No, no, of course, *terrible*. But come on—"

I had her attention. She was watching me now with interest, as if I had suggested the night could be painted some brighter color.

"I suppose it could have been worse," she said.

"Come on. I know it's bad, but look what we've done."

Anna sipped her drink carefully. "Are you saying it's been *fun*?"

"Yes, you know it's supposed to be *fun*."

"I've heard."

"Here's to fun."

We touched coffee cups and I felt the brandy as a warm flush. Anna rocked forward as she emptied her cup and the faint wedge of yellow slid to illuminate her eyes, her left breast, her hip.

"Well, I suppose . . ." I said.

She stared into her empty cup and then rocked back slowly and looked up at me.

"Yes."

But an idea had come to Anna. I could see it. I had no idea what, but I felt myself about to be drawn into a conspiracy—I could tell she was about to suggest something that broke the rules and the idea buoyed her heart, and before I even knew what it was, I was there.

"You know what we should do?" Anna said. "We should bring the paper to everyone working on the dikes."

The idea took a second to settle in my overheated brain.

"Deliver it by hand—"

"Yes."

"Just give it away—"

"Yes."

"—to *everybody* out there! To let them know—"

"*Yes!*"

And that was what we did. Todd was nervous when I told him to run three hundred extra copies, wanting to call Art or Louise to make sure it was okay, but I told him it wasn't necessary—I was the *editor*, dammit—and there was a certain unhinged exhilaration in saying that, especially since I was still coherent enough to be aware I really had no authority to spend more money on newsprint. It didn't matter. I was too taken with the idea to hesitate. Todd ran the extra copies, and we threw them into the back of the office pickup, and Anna and I drove them out to the war zone as the first light streaked a gray sky.

The men and women shoveling sand into bags, dirty faces the exhausted pallor of the water leaking through the dikes, looked at us with disbelief, as if we had woken them from a dream. They straightened slowly over their shovels, from their places in the line passing sandbags forward, from the side of the dike, and fumbled with the pages with numb, gloved hands. Then they were squinting at the pictures and elbowing each other, holding the paper out for a better look, handing copies back and forth, and it was only for a few minutes, of course, before they had to go back to work, but they held the paper and they smiled and laughed and frowned; they read bits aloud and pointed at people they recognized in photos. Anna and I stood to the side and every once in a while one of them looked up at us with a mixture of disbelief and awkward Midwestern gratitude.

We drove along the dikes dropping off copies every block or so, ending where the biggest battle was going on and the most people working. They took the paper and it was the same. They opened the pages; they read; they looked up. Some of them complained good-naturedly about their photos; some of them thanked us, but nobody had to say anything, really. Newspapers were folded and shoved in pockets, stuck inside jackets, carried to cars and trucks for safekeeping. Shovels scraped into gravel, bags passed from hand to hand with a heaviness you could feel from a distance, the air filled with plumes of breath, groans, and good-natured complaint. The river was still rising on the other side of the dike.

We were both exhausted and freezing. I felt Anna shivering against my shoulder and, maybe without even knowing, she leaned in to me for warmth. I became very aware of this, and felt myself doing the same. It was time to for us to go home, but we stood there, very gently leaning against each other for support, the last few copies still tucked under our arms, neither of us ready to leave.

Chapter 10

THE LAST ROUND OF DIKES HELD, more or less. There was a break that flooded a couple more houses and a vacant lot on the edge of town, but the river fell with the same swiftness with which it had risen, and the earth resurfaced, black and battered. The sky was such a psychotically cheerful blue that the memory of those gray days soon felt like a fever dream. Art looked a bit ashen when I told him about the three hundred extra copies, and the financially unfortunate fact that I had given them all away, but Louise was nodding so vigorously, he had little choice but to pretend it was a brilliant idea.

The town seemed quietly grateful. We were minor league heroes, at least in our own minds, and *The Shannon Sentinel* sailed into the summer with a giddy, light-headed, end-of-school feeling, even though of course for us there was no end of anything, just another issue to put out every Thursday night. It didn't matter. It felt easier. It felt less like work and more like some oddball calling, a thing all of us in that small office with desk chairs bumping up against each other were meant to be doing.

I noticed there were a couple of men, one a farmer, another a junior officer of some kind at the bank, who stopped by the front desk with excuses to talk to Anna. The farmer was shy and the bank officer spoke a little too much, but they both seemed kind and clearly interested. Anna listened, smiled, and maintained a kind of bland, polite distance that provided no encouragement whatsoever.

On a warm Thursday night with the doors propped open so we could enjoy a spring breeze heavy with the scent of the flowering apple tree in Art and Louise's yard across the street, I teased her about the men.

"That farmer. What's his name—Orville?—seems pretty nice."

"Orlin."

"Orlin? Jesus, Norwegians. Anyway, I think you could definitely do worse."

Anna stripped a border around a photograph and trimmed the tape neatly at the corner. "You do, do you?"

"Absolutely. Sweet and not bad-looking. Tall. That's always good, right? And look at the pickup truck he's driving. I'd say he's doing all right."

"Oh, I think he's doing just fine."

"Well . . . then. What's the problem here?"

"I am done with men."

She meant to say it lightly, but it didn't quite come off. The silence that always floated in the big, empty room settled around us.

"Really? All men? All three billion men on the planet—Chinese, Japanese, Indian, French, Norwegian, Irish, Portuguese? Short, tall, fat, skinny—"

"Definitely the Irish and Portuguese. I've never really cared for short or fat men, either."

"All right, we're narrowing the field. That's fine. Choosy is good. But that still leaves—wait, let me do the math—one-point-six billion men."

She still hadn't looked up. "I think you've got the decimal off. I think it's one-point-six men."

"Really?"

"Yes, you better watch your decimals. Remember, that's what got Stacy in trouble."

For some reason I couldn't let it go. "I don't know. We can't all be that bad."

"No one really believes how bad you can be," Anna said. She stepped back to consider her finished page, flexing the fingers in her right hand with a barely visible wince. She had early onset arthritis, one of a series of health problems I would discover over time. She was never well, really, when I knew her.

"Come on," I said. "I was just—"

"You know I was married."

The flat declaration of that statement, too, bothered me in a way I didn't quite understand.

"Well, yes. The kids—"

"The kids. Yes. Well, it didn't go so well."

"But it was just one marriage."

"It was enough."

"But it's the modern age—marriages are like hats, you try

them on until you find the one you like," said the twenty-year-old with no experience trying on multiple hats or marriages.

"Really? Is that how it works now?" And again, it was a little too sharp. I wished I could rewind this conversation and start over.

"Absolutely," I said, because it seemed the best bet was to hurry past whatever was going on.

"Here's how it worked for me, Eric. The first time I left, I came back after a week. I told myself it was just for a day. I had the baby to care for, and I had to get everything together. I left her with a friend in Bismarck, and I came back. He—we—had been living in this trailer out in the country and, when I came back, he called my mother and father, and they drove out to try to convince me to give him another chance. They're Catholic, you know, and he always charmed them; he always helped out . . ."

She laid a fresh sheet of paper on the light table and bent toward the faint blue lines on the empty page, her perfect profile lit from below, her eyes reflecting the color of a clouded lake.

"They tell me I have to give him a second chance; he knows he's made some mistakes, but he's promised to change. He's going to change. He's really going to change. He's gone out while they're talking and when they leave he comes back. He asks me if I'm going to give him another chance."

She fumbled at the edge of the table and found her coffee cup. The strips of copy were arranged on the table beside the empty page but she hadn't touched them.

"I said I would. He said good, I could cook him dinner. He knew I didn't like blood. I have *trouble* with blood. So he goes out the front door and he gets this big slab of meat from something he had killed, a deer, or an elk, and he slaps it on the table in front of me. Cook this, he says, and he goes back out the door. I'm trying to cut up this bloody meat in the sink and I can hear my parents saying I have to stay with him, I have to give him a chance, and it just seems so absurd, it's funny. It seems like it's happening to someone else. My little girl is in Bismarck and I'm cutting up this bloody meat . . . and I look down and I've cut the tip off my finger."

Anna held up her left hand. I'd never noticed that the ring finger was flattened and slightly shorter.

"It's bleeding—really badly—but you can't tell. It's all mixed up with the stupid bloody meat that's impossible to cut, and it just seems so absurd. I don't even stop. I just keep hacking away. I wrap it all up, the blood, fingertip. I fry it up. He eats it. Doesn't even notice. Doesn't notice I'm bleeding. Doesn't notice *anything*."

She had gone back to work, placing the first strip of copy on the page. I watched her, the movements always simple and precise, no wasted motion. A kind of artistry.

"Little girl?" I said. "Your son is older."

She shook her head, pulled the strip off the page, and repasted it.

"What did I say? My son. My oldest."

If you are a journalist, which is what I've been for a long time now, lots of people will tell you their stories, and you will forget almost all of them. The ones you remember live in a particular detail, an image or incident that carves its place in your memory. Anna had told me nothing about her marriage before, and now it would be forever fixed to a vision of her bent over a sink full of raw meat, pummeling away at it helplessly, losing a piece of herself in the effort. That evening I only knew I had presumed too much, carried a joke too far.

"Listen, I—"

"Remember that night you were talking about America's wars?" Anna asked with her small smile.

I felt a flush of embarrassment and nodded.

"Marriage was my Vietnam, Eric. Never again."

Chapter 11

IN THE BRIEF SPRING THAT WAS LEFT before summer, the high school held its graduation and we went together, Anna to take pictures, me to interview students for the story. The ceremony was in the gym, then the newly minted graduates of Shannon High School filed outside onto the grass to shake hands and accept congratulations. Caps had been thrown in the air earlier and they were bareheaded now in their dark blue robes. Mostly blondes and coppery redheads, the descendants of phlegmatic Norwegian and Swedish farmers and Irish railroad workers, lightly carrying the bright crowns of their youth on this day of sun-filled promise.

One of the boys said something to Anna. He seemed to know her son Stephen, although Stephen was much younger. I watched her stiffen slightly, a moment of awkwardness and something that seemed to resemble fear, and then I heard her laugh. She took his hand and placed it lightly on her hip, taking the other one in her own, and they took a sudden graceful turn around the grass while the kids nearby in line applauded.

"That was a waltz?" I said when she wandered over after I had finished my interviews.

"What? Oh, that. More or less." She laughed and I was surprised by the happiness in her voice.

"He lives down the street and he used to babysit for me a couple of years ago, when Stephen was too young to take care of his sister." Anna hesitated. "He caught me dancing one night, and I promised I'd teach him."

"*Caught* you dancing? It's a crime in North Dakota?"

"Not if you polka."

"Seriously."

"Caught me dancing. Alone."

"Wait—what? Does that mean—I mean—is that a metaphor?"

Anna was staring at me as if I had started speaking Chinese. She blinked and blushed. "Dancing, Eric. *Dancing*. He left and realized he had left his jacket and when he came back he didn't knock and I was dancing alone in the living room. And . . . it was embarrassing to both of us, but I told him I'd teach him someday." She smiled. "He reminded me I never had."

"Okay. Wait, he caught you waltzing?"

Some parents Anna knew came by and she shook their hands and congratulated them.

"Not really."

"What, then?"

"Just dancing."

I became suspicious. "To what?"

"Well, uhmm . . . Bread."

"*Bread*."

"Yes, Bread, the band. You remember Bread?"

"Oh, yes, I remember *Bread*. Which song?"

"Does it matter?"

"It really, really does."

"I believe it was 'Lost Without Your Love.'"

"You believe it was."

"It's just a song."

"You were dancing alone to 'Lost Without Your Love'?"

She waved briefly at someone on the far end of the high school lawn.

"I was dancing alone to 'Lost Without Your Love.' Are you happy?"

"I am. Much is becoming clear to me."

"Oh, I'm sure it is. Men don't dance alone, I know."

"Sure we do. We go crazy. But to Led Zeppelin or the Who. 'Won't Get Fooled Again.' Rock and roll."

That made her smile.

"That's not dancing. That's just exercise. Jumping around."

"Well, yeah. *Dancing*."

Anna considered me with a look that was already becoming familiar, as if I had handed her a small, unexpected present.

"I can hardly wait for the next Christmas party," she said.

"So you never taught him?"

A faint stiffness came into her posture. "No, of course not."

Done with men. Done with men of all ages, young and old. But dancing to Bread.

"They were a truly terrible band," I said.

"They were," Anna said. "And they were *great*."

The reception line was breaking up and she stepped onto

the grass to take a shot of three girls skipping onto the grass, then running, one holding her mortar board, their hair all flying back, their blue robes flaring as if they might be about to take flight. Radiant and slightly dazed smiles. The exhilaration of an end and simultaneous beginning.

I remembered that feeling. It really hadn't been that long, and for a brief moment, I could feel again the sense of stepping out into an infinite future, of freeing yourself from something big you didn't quite understand to reach toward a buoyant, half-formed image of something even larger, brighter.

"Freedom."

Their backs were to us now, figures framed in a trot across fields of green and blue, robes ballooning behind them. Anna snapped a quick series of final shots.

"For today," Anna said, but I could see they made her happy.

We walked back to the office together. The day was clear, warm. I had started the morning by throwing on my first polo shirt of the season, but Anna wore a long-sleeve blouse tucked into black jeans.

"You don't like the sun much, I guess."

"I love the sun," she said. "I love days like this. I love spring. I *love* summer."

I glanced down at her long sleeves and, as she noticed, she tugged one of them slightly farther down.

"I burn easily," she said.

Down the sidewalk Art and Louise were heading home. They walked as they always did, side by side, a couple of feet separating them, as if they each had a small bubble of self-contained space.

They only very rarely touched each other. No hugs. *Old people*, I thought.

Louise was half a head taller than her husband and every third step or so, she took a small half step to stay beside him. It was a surprisingly girlish skip, and it made us both smile.

"I've been informed that there are no worthwhile men on the planet and you're officially done with us," I said, because I am the kind of person who cannot help but touch a sore tooth. "But how can you resist that kind of happiness?"

I thought Anna hadn't heard me, but she was fixed on what was happening ahead of us. Art and Louise had stopped and were facing each other, maintaining the same slightly formal distance, the half-moon of his stomach pointing at the cliff wall of her hips. Art was talking and Louise did not look happy. She looked as if something were being taken from her, cruelly and for no reason.

"It's just a chance to escape," I heard Art say. "I need it now and then."

We slowed as we approached. Anna said to me, a little too loudly, "The tradition is a kegger out by the river. High school kids."

"Okay," I said, only mildly baffled before also speaking loudly. "I guess we won't worry about it, then."

Art turned and fixed us with a gentle smile. "They've been doing it for a hundred years, and every senior class somehow thinks it's a secret. There's a glen down by the river. I still remember our graduation party. Don't you, Louise?"

There was something slightly broken in her gaze and she struggled for a moment before managing to rearrange her features into their customary Mount Rushmore–like visage. "Hell, yes. Bobby McIntyre tried to pick me up."

"I'm sure he did," Art said. "He's in prison now, I believe."

They started walking with us.

"That was Bobby's career path from day one," Louise said. "I think we voted him most likely to commit a class-one felony."

"Now, dear, I'm pretty sure we didn't even know what a class-one felony was," Art said.

"Ah, the innocence of youth," I said, and, yes, I understood why they all laughed. Or I did after a moment, anyway.

We strolled to the office, where Art and Louise peeled off to their small house across the street, still in their individual bubbles of space, like friendly strangers on a long journey.

"What was that about?" I asked quietly.

They were too far away to hear us, but Anna waited until the door shut behind them. She glanced sideways at me. "How can I resist, Eric? Really?"

"Okay," I said. "Now you really have to tell me what we're talking about."

She had a surprisingly throaty laugh; maybe it was all the cigarettes and coffee. "No, I don't," she said. "There are some things you have to figure out for yourself."

I would, but on that clement May afternoon, with the light hanging in the air as if suspended in time, I was briefly stuck in place. Anna walked on ahead of me, her trim figure moving with its farm-girl sense of purpose, as I tried to sort out the afternoon: what I had just missed, yes, but more than that, this woman who was done with men turning so beautifully on the grass while all the boys applauded.

Chapter 12

SHANNON WAS TURNING 120 THAT SUMMER, and a three-day celebration was planned, the kind of party small towns are always throwing for themselves: an all-class high school reunion, a carnival, a downtown street fair, and a host of silly contests: best beard, best old-fashioned dress, best authentic-period kid's costume. It was still a couple of months away, but Louise and Art were deeply involved in the planning, so the *Sentinel* was already running breathless weekly updates, written by Louise after a couple of stiff shots of sixty-proof inspiration.

I had started to make changes in the paper. Nothing major, a loosening of the rules: a photo spread of the last day of school stretched across the top of the front page, a long story on the damage to the city drainage system from the flood and the city's difficult options, both lighter stuff and more serious stuff. I had no articulated vision, no master plan. I was just doing what felt right and trying to have fun because Louise was right, it was supposed to be *fun*. Looking back, I would say if I had any governing idea it was an aversion to the deadly middle—the great middle space of dully responsible journalism, the county commission and city council reports, the pro forma stories of every kind. We couldn't abandon them completely, but I cut back to the minimum required for civic responsibility. I had earned a measure of trust from Louise and even ever-fretful Art with the coverage of the flood, and with the careless profligacy of youth I spent it on whatever caught my fancy.

The middle space is a good place to hide, and I was worried Anna, who'd found comfortable invisibility in the least inspiring work, wouldn't like her new assignments. But I think she did. If nothing else, they got her out of the office. She had a natural eye as a photographer, and when I discovered that, I sent her out with the paper's battered Nikon more often. Sometimes on a beautiful day, with nothing much pressing on us, I would send her out with orders no more specific than to come back with something good.

She always did. The town going about its lazy summer business. A sweet-faced bag boy at the grocery store helping to load the car for an older couple caught leaning against each other with the quiet intimacy of age. A fish at the end of a line, frozen above the mirrored surface of the man-made lake at the edge of Shannon. The men at the Midwestern Forge factory, lined up outside the entrance with their cigarettes burning holes in the dusk. Not that it was all mood and revelation. We ran pictures of children, always plenty of children doing adorable things, and the occasional pet, too. Wet dogs were a big winner; a dog in a kiddy pool with some kids was absolute gold. We were a small-town newspaper, after all.

Those were my days—a job I had stumbled into, a temporary occupation, I was sure, but one that kept me busy enough. The nights were where a sense of purposelessness sometimes stole back into my head like an unpleasant friend settling into your favorite chair.

Todd and I started playing pool on a regular basis at the Buffalo Bar, especially on the nights after the paper had been printed. We were evenly matched and played each other or as a team against the old men who felt as much a part of the Buffalo as the scuffed stools and cracked mirror behind the bar. They always beat us, but we were good enough to make it close.

Todd had abandoned vacuum cleaners, but had taken up model trains with a kind of unblinking focus that was slightly unnerving. Some nights we watched the Twins in his living room with a miniature Baldwin Class R steam locomotive circling the furniture, the yellow light at the front chasing past the steep bluffs of the couch, the torturous turn by the ottoman, the floating alien spaceship of the television, round and round and round, while Todd and I sat in the dark and watched Gary Gaetti launch another ball high into the artificial twilight.

We waited in suspended disbelief. An outfielder raced toward the wall. The train chugged through the dark. In the stands, bodies rose, hands reached toward a spot of white. A roar erupted in some distant Elysian field. The train's bright eye searched the corners of the room.

. . .

I WAS BENT OVER the pool table, focused on a gleaming crescent sliver of the seven ball, when Anna stepped into the light around the table. She was with her friend Christina, the waitress at the café. I knew Anna's son was old enough to take care of his sister and Anna did go out every so often, but I was still surprised to see her at the Buff, an establishment where both Todd and I were considered such reputable citizens we were allowed to run bar tabs. I pulled back the cue and missed.

"Tough shot," she said.

"Not really."

"Well, tough enough, I guess, huh, champ?" Christina said, winking at Todd, who smiled shyly and sank the eight ball, ending our game.

We played partners, the four of us—Anna and I the "college team," as Christina called us. Anna played better than I would have thought, leaning over and considering each move carefully, her dark eyes catching a reflection from the narrow lamp above the table as if a piece of lost silver were reflecting up from the bottom of a whiskey-colored pool.

She made some nice shots, but Christina had clearly been born on a pool table. She was too good, and Todd coasted in her wake as they beat us three straight times.

"All that education and you still can't find a side pocket," Christina said as we sat down at the bar and let the old men have the table for a while. She had wheat-blond, razor-straight hair she kept pushed back behind her ears in a kind of too-busy-to-worry-about-it cut. She was trim and athletic-looking, taller than Anna, the kind of outdoorsy Dakota farm girl who has been through just enough to pretend to lose her illusions.

"I'm not a side pocket kind of guy," I said. "Straight and true is my motto."

"Of course it is," she said, turning to Todd. "Men are uncomplicated creatures, don't you think?"

"I have no idea," Todd said, sipping his beer a little too quickly.

"There you are," Christina said. "Did I ever tell you I like your tattoo?"

Anna was watching her. Anna, the watcher. She saw me watching her watch and, as Todd flexed his tattooed bicep to Christina's admiration, smiled. "Are there any uncomplicated people?"

"Billions."

"Really?"

"Well, at least two."

"Heard that," Christina said, and then to Todd: "Can you make him jump by popping your muscle?"

Anna choked on her beer and, as she raised her hand to cover her mouth, her long sleeve slipped, and I saw briefly a perfect white circle of skin around her wrist, as if it had been kept from the sunlight forever.

. . .

I KNEW BY NOW that her marriage had been bad and I knew that she had been hurt by it. But I'd heard only a very little more. They ran away when Anna was just barely seventeen and were married in South Dakota by a justice of the peace. The strange thing is my parents did the same thing, but then they rode on out of the Great Plains, taking the Greyhound bus down to Las Vegas and on to the bright promise of Los Angeles. When they finally came back the world had opened up, and it would never close down again, despite all the years teaching at a small private school in a small Minnesota city. They had seen beyond the pencil-drawn Midwestern horizon and came back because they knew their home from both inside and out now, and they still loved it.

But Anna and her new husband, barely a year and a half older than she was, turned around and came back to the oil fields two days later. The company had trailers scattered throughout the country, situated so the men could keep an eye on the equipment in the staging yards tossed up alongside the narrow dirt roads that snaked off to the wells. They were given one of those.

Wild and lonely country, country burned long ago into Anna's blood, but lonely country at night in a beat-to-crap oil company trailer. No one else around for miles. The sky and the broken, brown land, tossed up like a jumble of old teeth. Was she happy? Was this what she wanted, this brief stretch and snap back to the same small abandoned patch of the universe she had known since birth? I have no idea, but they were young and they had the passion of youth to keep them busy in their tin bedroom, and in no time at all she was pregnant. The fact that she wasn't pregnant before they were married, that no baby came from the inevitable fumbling in the back of his Firebird, was probably the true miracle in the marital equation. But they were having a baby before they knew it, and because they had chosen to be married and could still believe they were making a life together, it came without guilt or confusion, at least for Anna. She told me once that the news she was having her first child was the most uncomplicated moment of happiness she could remember.

Anna and the baby, alone most of the day and much of the night, when her husband worked late and then drove into town with the men for a drink or two or three. (Again, another similarity: like me at the paper, he was underage, but no one carded a worker in the oil fields.) Anna and the baby, alone in the trailer, which was situated in a fingernail crease of a valley between a pair of buttes that rose to seal off most of the sky. A narrow stream gathered at the bottom of the valley. In the spring, when the land was flush with Indian paintbrush and wild blue flax, Anna cleared a plot to the east, so it caught the rising sun, and planted a garden. She tended carrots, onions, lettuce, snap peas, and a few miniature watermelons, while the baby lay happily on a blanket spread in the prairie grass.

Long days and just the two of them, and often at dusk the sound of the coyotes calling to each other from the ridges, a call so high and clear it felt like it could carry halfway around the world, and she sat on the metal steps, the baby in her arms, and knew she and her child were the only ones listening. Was she happy? I believe she was happy that summer.

. . .

WE STEPPED OUT onto the street together outside the Buffalo Bar and Christina was leaning slightly against Todd, who was trying to take it all in stride and not doing a very good job of it. Anna and I stood awkwardly off to the side. For the last half hour she had been worried about getting home to her kids and had fallen silent.

"Well," I said, "the best thing about the Buffalo Bar is I live right across the street. Good night, ladies and gentlemen."

The evening was unexpectedly warm. The first night of summer. I took a step and lingered. A car turned onto Main Street on the far side of the railroad tracks and headed the other direction, the taillights a pair of curious eyes slowly receding. Anna watched the car with the oddly attentive regret I had come to recognize. Her hands were held pensively beneath her chin and she was unconsciously holding her sleeves up again. The white circle, a scar of some kind, I had to believe, floated in my memory as clearly as a full moon.

"See you, college boy," Christina said, still leaning against Todd. "Better practice your pool."

My own footsteps echoed in my ears. "Eric," Anna said, when I was halfway across the street. She had caught up to me by the time I turned, and stood a little too close, her eyes large in the dark. "It was just an accident," she said very quietly. "I'll tell you about it sometime."

And, still holding her sleeve, Anna briefly pressed a hand against my chest, as if to seal a secret there.

Chapter 13

SUMMER IS THE SEASON OF REDEMPTION in North Dakota, repayment for the brutal winters. The endless sunlight slants across the last hours of the day in a benediction and it's hard to feel too bad about anything. Riding this sunstruck wave of senseless optimism, the *Sentinel* barreled into the town's anniversary celebration, so ceaselessly tooting the horn of civic self-promotion that the stories began to resemble a parade of drunken Shriners on Bourbon Street. Louise led the parade with a front-page weekly column that, at its best, had a kind of majestic, inebriated swagger, and, at its worst, a lot of typos.

Beneath the euphoria lay a ton of work for all of us, but especially for Edith Swenson, the woman who handled the social notes. She was inundated with notices of family and class reunions, pancake breakfasts, special church services, charity auctions, and even the schedule for an evening of cowboy poetry, hosted by a local resident who had written four hundred rhyming couplets celebrating the Glories of All God's Creation, with a particular focus on livestock.

Edith stood very erect and had admirably broad shoulders. Her voice was as parched as a dust bowl wind and she was so unflappable that a tornado landing in the middle of an earthquake during an asteroid strike might just possibly have caused her to cock an eyebrow. Still, the demands of her good neighbors started to weigh on her. She was sixty-something years old and she took to joining us at the Buffalo Bar at the end of the working week, ordering a whiskey neat and drinking it down as if it were weak tea.

She was standing at the bar on a Friday when I slid in beside her to order another beer.

"Looking good, kid. Nobody's even figured out you're underage yet."

This was mildly disconcerting, especially while waiting for Bernie, the owner, to serve me.

"I appreciate you keeping that quiet. Particularly now."

Edith had the driest smile I had ever seen on a woman. Give her a fedora and she could have been Humphrey Bogart.

"Don't worry. You've earned a drink or two."

My Schmidt arrived unasked-for. It struck me that perhaps I had been spending a little too much time here.

"You, too."

"Parties," she said, with the tone of a medieval surgeon contemplating leprosy.

"You've lived here forever, right?"

Her eyes swiveled to contemplate me.

"Wait. I don't mean—"

"Since the beginning of time."

"Sorry, I just wondered, do you remember when Anna started at the paper?"

I saw her hesitation.

"She's doing a *great* job," I said. "Really good. I was just curious, really. How she got started."

"It wasn't that long ago." Edith frowned. "Well, maybe it was. The years run together. She was just in the office one day, sitting at a desk, doing her work. I don't remember Art or Louise hiring her." She smiled. "Maybe she just showed up and sat down. I remember Louise started giving her everything to proofread. That's what she was at first, a proofreader. We needed a proofreader . . . She's a good speller," Edith concluded with admiration.

Todd was playing pool with one of the old men. They finished and he glanced my way to see if I was up next. I shook my head. Anna had been coming to the bar a bit more often, usually when the office gathered, and I had looked when I first came in, hoping to see her, but she wasn't here tonight.

"She is a good speller," I said. "She's a good photographer. She does a lot of things well."

Edith considered me. "I imagine she's glad you figured that out."

"It just seems . . . odd. I don't think she ever had a journalism class or anything like that. I just wondered what made her try the *Sentinel*."

I wondered much more than that, actually. I wondered how she ended up in Shannon. I wondered what sent her this way and why she only came this far. I wondered about her second child, her daughter, after things had so clearly gone bad after the first. And I wondered why I wondered, why these questions had come to matter so much to me.

"Ask her. I think she's got stories, that one."

"Sure."

"You're doing a good job, kiddo." Edith returned to her contemplation of the liquor bottles behind the bar. "You better be careful. That's when you get trapped."

. . .

THE LAST NIGHT of the anniversary celebration was the last night of the carnival, the night of the fireworks, the night we could see the end to a crazy week of work. Anna and I took all the photos we could during the day, more than we could use early in the night, and then we were really done. It was Saturday and the paper wouldn't come out for six days, so we had plenty of time to write, plenty of time to get everything together. I interviewed a few of the people streaming through the midway, just to be sure we had more than enough color, and we were all free. Todd, Christina, and I wandered the streets like sailors on leave.

The carnival had been set up on Main Street, the midway running past the bank, the rides scattered all the way back to the railroad tracks, lighting up the sky with spinning circles and blinking towers of Christmas-colored lights, the noise echoing between the buildings, a wheezing and groaning calliope, the whistles and bangs of the game booths, the hoarse shouts of the barkers, and, somewhere on the edge of the celebration, a fire engine siren starting and stopping over and over in fits of either ecstasy or panic.

Anna showed up with her kids as the sun set. Stephen was blond and pale, tall and slender for his age. He had feathery hair, oddly perfect oyster-shell ears, and the somber reserve of an oldest child pressed into early responsibility. His little sister, Samantha, called Sam by everyone, was the surprise: red curls, a mad archipelago of freckles across her cheeks, and electric-green eyes constantly searching the world for trouble. She held her mother's hand reluctantly, leaning toward the midway.

"Nice hat," Anna said.

Todd had attended the cowboy poetry reading, apparently of his own free will, and brought me back a straw cowboy hat with *Reading, Riding, wRiting* circling a white band around the crown. I tipped the brim. "Thank you kindly, ma'am."

Stephen's gaze locked on the Slingshot, a ride that looked like a big hammer and spun you completely upside down. He looked like he wished he could ride it right out of here into orbit.

"You wanna do it?" Todd asked. "I can't get anybody to go with me."

"That's because you're going to throw up," Christina said. She had her own cowboy hat, a black felt model she wore tilted back.

"What do you think?" Todd said.

Stephen blinked hard a couple of times. "Let's do it!"

They charged toward the line as if jumping off a cliff. Seated and strapped into place in the hammer's head, they laughed as the ride began to swing back and forth, rising higher and higher with each arc, until it stood completely on end, and they hung upside down for a long, teetering moment—Todd screaming louder than Stephen—before swinging all the way around.

They traced several rapid, complete circles, their shouts of joy and terror rising and falling in synchronicity.

"This is the part where you step back out of range," Christina said.

"Todd has an iron stomach," I said. "I've seen him eat five-day-old pizza."

Christina's eyes circled with the ride.

"Don't want to think about that now." She glanced at Anna. "How about Stephen?"

"Well. He's never really liked heights."

"Perfect."

They went around a few more times and then the Slingshot rocked itself back to earth. Todd came out first and promptly sat, or perhaps fell, down. Stephen ran toward Anna with his skinny arms held high. "That was awesome! Let's do it again! Mom, you want to come? It's great! Come on!"

He charged across the street and pulled up just short of wrapping Anna in an excited hug, remembering he was twelve. He stood awkwardly in front of her, wanting to share his triumph and keep his cool at the same time, and Anna was suddenly a real mother to me, a mother knowing enough not to reach out and touch him.

"I could *never* do that, Stephen. But it looked like fun."

Christina was bent over Todd.

"How you doing, cowboy?"

"Stop moving and I'll tell you."

"Come over here. Lay down on the bench."

"Yes."

Sam tugged harder at her mom's hand.

"I want to go on a ride. I want to go on the Octopus!"

"I can take her," said Stephen, grizzled carnival-ride veteran.

Anna smiled and handed him the tickets. His sister refused to take his hand but followed him in the direction of the whirling metal monster down the street. Anna's eyes tracked them until they were safely in line.

"Well," I said. "Your turn. The Ferris wheel? The funhouse?"

Anna was watching the Ferris wheel tumble to a stop at the far end of the carnival, a bright cyclops eye peering over the town. She was wearing a simple white blouse, unbuttoned at the collar, that seemed to glow against her skin, accenting the curve of her neck and the hollow where the material gapped at the swell of her breasts. She ran her fingers absently along the opening.

"It's just a small-town carnival, really," she said.

"Come on, it's not so bad."

"Yes, it's the Seattle World's Fair."

"Okay. It's pretty small."

"Tiny."

"Hardly there at all."

Anna hugged herself, somehow managing to hold her sleeves in place. "When these things came to Bowman when I was a kid, they were such a big deal. We were excited for days before they arrived. You'd get one night you could go and your parents would give you a dollar for tickets."

"A dollar! What did that buy? One ride?"

"It bought four rides. It bought a trip on the Ferris wheel, the Tilt-A-Whirl, the Octopus, and then you had to decide. You had one more, and there probably weren't more than three or four other rides, but you had to choose. You could go on one more ride, or you could go to one of the booths and try to win a prize."

"What did you do?"

"I always took my shot at the prize. That was my weakness."

"Ever win anything?"

"A rubber alligator. About this big." She held her hands about six inches apart.

"That's not so bad. They're all rigged, you know."

Stephen and Sam had arrived at the front of the line and they ran through the harsh light toward their car on the Octopus. Sam waved wildly as it rose into the air. Anna waved back.

"Are you telling me life's not fair, Eric?"

"I am," said the very young man who still believed that, in the end, it would all work out. "Or at least carnivals."

The game booths were behind us and we turned to consider the people playing. Someone tossed something toward a blur of yellow and there was a collective groan.

"Life's not fair," Anna said. "The funny thing is, I still don't want to believe it."

"Come on. I'll show you."

I took her arm and pulled her to the nearest booth, where a group of small orange ducks floated in a tin tub painted blue to resemble a pond. The carny was older, tattoos along his arms faded like newsprint left out in the sun. He considered us as if we were a pair of dying fish at the bottom of an aquarium.

"Three tosses for a dollar. You ring a duck and you win a prize."

"Just one duck? One dollar?"

"Yep."

I fished in my pocket. "You know, you used to be able to get four rides for a dollar. The Ferris wheel, the Tilt-A-Whirl, even the *Octopus*."

He shrugged shoulders so thin they could have served as surgical instruments. "There's no justice in or out of court, boss. You want to play or not?"

"I want to play."

The three rings were hard plastic. I held the first one in my hand.

"See, it looks easy, but they're just a little too small, a little too hard, and the ducks are bobbing, so—"

Without looking, I tossed the ring toward the tub, where it settled perfectly around a duck's neck.

"You were saying, Einstein?" The carny pulled a good-sized teddy bear off the shelf and handed it to Anna, who hesitated and then took it with a short, disbelieving laugh, considering me as if I had just landed from another planet.

"You're wrong," I said, "you clearly have *incredibly* good luck."

Anna held the bear out, moving it from side to side so it seemed to be shaking its head. I couldn't tell if it made her happy or sad.

"That's your luck, Eric. Not mine."

"I don't think so. Anyway, it's your bear."

"Or Sam's." She managed a smile. "I think my teddy bear days have passed."

"Or Sam's, then."

"Thank you."

We walked back to a spot where we could see the rides. The Octopus had come to a stop. I felt our time together ticking away.

"You never told me what happened to your wrist," I said.

"Both wrists, Eric." She held up her left arm, the other arm, and let the sleeve fall. In the darkness I couldn't really see anything, but she seemed to think it glowed. "And, no, I didn't."

"Okay. I just—"

"I know. Maybe someday. Is that okay?"

The kids arrived as a blur, Samantha tackling her mother's waist and swinging as if still on the ride. "That was fun!"

Anna held on to her daughter as if she might spin off into orbit.

"Look. Mr. Valery won you a bear."

Sam gave it a glance. "Can we go on the Ferris wheel, Mom? Can we, please? Please?"

"I think we can all ride in one car," Stephen said. "Sam hardly counts as a person."

"Maybe *you* hardly count!"

"You both count, but I bet we can squeeze in together." Anna put one hand on her son's shoulder, completing the connection between the three of them. In the darkness I couldn't read her expression, but the faint sadness I had first seen as I handed her the bear hung in her voice, weighing down her effort to sound buoyant. She let go of Sam briefly to push her hair into place and I could see she was determined this would pass before her children noticed.

Anna turned to me and there was an odd cant to her body, as though she were balancing on something unsteady.

"Would you like to come with us?"

The children stared up at me in surprise. And I wanted to, more than made sense, but they were a family and Stephen and Sam were little kids and this was a carnival.

"That's all right. I should find Todd."

Her eyes seemed very wide and very dark in the carnival light. She fashioned a smile.

"You probably should. God knows what they've been up to."

Anna and her kids walked down the crowded street holding hands, slowly turning into a set of cutout black paper dolls connected at the wrists. Half a block away Anna whispered to her daughter.

Sam turned and shouted, "Thank you, Mr. Eric!"—waving the flop-armed bear hard enough to dismember it. They disappeared around a corner and I stood in the middle of the cacophony and cartoon lights suddenly feeling very alone.

Todd had recovered sufficiently that he and Christina could join me in the beer garden. We stood at a plank bar and everyone came by, Edith, Art and Louise, members of the city council, lifers from the Buffalo Bar, everyone, and everyone liked my cowboy hat and everyone was happy and triumphant and relieved and drinking too much and the carnival grew louder and then fireworks were exploding overhead in the colors of the American flag and they were brilliant, blinding, too loud, and invisible ash was drifting down through the night, landing on your shoulders, in your hair, and the lights were out and Todd and Christina had stolen away and the bartender was looking across the rough-sawn bar, saying, *Time to go home, cowboy.*

• • •

I WAS STANDING at the window of my apartment, looking at the labyrinth of shadows on the now-deserted street, and the more I stared, the more complicated and confused it seemed, a geometry of hidden spaces and crosshatched lines, lighter patches of gray like doors opening into nothing, triangles and bars of perfect black cutting off every escape. There was a terrible precision to the pattern, as if the nature of the carnival could only be revealed when the lights had gone out and all motion had ceased.

A flicker on the glass caught the corner of my eye and I looked up to see small creatures of light swarming in a playful tangle down the block. I was lost until I realized the carousel was being taken down and I was watching flashlights dance along the metal poles and ghostly wooden horses. A feeling that had been bothering me since Anna disappeared with her children, a sense of something essential escaping my grasp, something I needed to understand, settled on me like a final cinder of ash.

I'll tell you about it someday, she'd said. Yes, there was that. But something more.

The dancing lights climbed into the air again, moving in a collapsing circle in the night as another ride came down. It was like watching a constellation disassembled. The disappearing form of the familiar world.

The phone on the wall rang. I looked at the clock radio on the counter. It was 2:14 a.m., and I don't believe in this kind of thing, but it is a small, enduring mystery in my life that I knew they were calling to tell me my father had died.

Chapter 14

I WOULD HAVE SAID I HAD NOTHING from Anna, no letters, keepsakes, photographs, nothing beyond a few old copies of *The Shannon Sentinel*, buried somewhere in a banker's box in the storage room. But I was cleaning out a different box a few years back, a jumble of stuff from all the moves early in my working life, and I came across a framed picture she had taken.

The photograph was of Shannon, taken from some distance outside of town at dusk, a full moon hanging in the sky above the grain elevators and water tower like a magic coin of good fortune. A timed exposure. Beautifully done. I was sure Anna's eye had been behind the lens. I had no memory of deciding to keep the picture or framing it, but as I held it up into the light, I remembered the photograph appearing out of nothingness in the developing tray at the *Sentinel*.

Anna and I had been in the darkroom. I was teaching her how to develop and print photographs. These are nearly lost and largely useless talents these days, but this was when every photographer still retired to a curtained closet or windowless room to discover what suspended moments of life had been captured on each roll of film.

She was a natural photographer, but no one had ever taught her what to do in the darkroom, so I showed her how to mix the chemicals, spool the thirty-five-millimeter film into the circular wire guide that fit inside the canister, and let it develop. This was all housekeeping. The magical part came when you chose your shot and threaded it into the enlarger, placed the blank sheet of photo paper in the easel, and flipped the light to expose the frame.

There was the sudden, always beautiful appearance of the image on the paper, then the moment in the developing tray when the picture crawled back out of its brief sleep and took permanent form, the baths in the stop solution and fixer, and finally the photographs clipped at odd angles on the line, cubist scraps of the world hung out to dry like laundry. All of this satisfying, no matter how flawed the photographs themselves, a brief sense of creation, life out of nothingness, form out of darkness.

But there had been something else that day—something earlier that led us to retreat to the darkroom. Art had been showing one of his friends around the office. There was a piece of new equipment in the back shop. I can't remember what, but Art was a big man in a small town with a social circle in which everyone seemed to have known each other since kindergarten. He liked to show off his new stuff. A kind of ceremony attended the visits from Art's old friends, men his age, or sometimes a little younger. He stood taller, which elevated his belly, as if it were trying to fill in for his birdlike chest. A faint pink glow came into his round cheeks and his hands became even more nervous, quicker to take someone by the arm, holding on a little too long as he steered them from one room to another. Louise was never around for these visitations. She usually showed up later in the day, her own glow not quite so healthy, but just as hearty and far more redolent of either brandy or whiskey. On this afternoon, Art had finished the tour and was walking out the door with the owner of the funeral home, a slight and aristocratic silver-haired man with the rubbery pallor of someone who spent long days breathing in formaldehyde fumes, when they intersected with Louise marching up the sidewalk.

Anna and I were the only people in the newsroom. I was leaning over Anna's desk to read something on her typewriter, and they were clearly visible in the window directly in front of us. They all stopped and there was this awkward pirouette as Art's embalmed friend stepped quickly onto the grass to give Louise free passage and, with a strangely formal wave, hurried on down the sidewalk. Louise faced Art and, before she spoke, he glanced awkwardly at the window.

I was wondering if he could see us in the reflection of the June day on the glass when Anna spoke.

"You were going to show me how to develop pictures? Now would be a good time."

We stepped together through the revolving metal door into darkness lit only by the single red light. The darkroom was little more than a closet, really, a long narrow space with shelves full of chemicals and a bench with the developing trays along one wall. The enlarger squatted by itself along the other wall.

"What was that about?" I asked.

She was leaning against the bench and my eyes were still adjusting to the dark, but I was aware of the hesitation, the stillness before her head moved imperceptibly from side to side.

"I don't know," she said. "Show me what to do."

We went through the preliminaries and then came the first exposure, which was a little too dark, and I remember I was showing Anna how to lighten parts of a print by dodging, moving something, even your hand, back and forth above the paper; I was holding her hand at the wrist, leaning over her shoulder, and I could feel her pulse through her skin. Breathing, heartbeats, the warmth of someone's skin, these things are more intimate parts of us than any words we say, any promises we make. For a moment I lost myself in the accelerated tick of her heart and when I returned my attention to the photograph it was too late.

"We've ruined it," I said. "We have to try again. You do it this time."

I stood back and watched her lighten the clouds across the top of the frame. Her hands were small and translucent in the light. She kept her nails short. Her fingers floated, slightly separated, above the reappearing sky, and there was something so vulnerable about this.

"You're a natural," I said.

She pulled her hand back and switched off the exposure. Her eyes rose from the print and the gratitude burning in them unsettled me. It was as if I had shown her fire.

"I love it. Thank you."

"All right. Good. I'll show you the rest."

We stood side by side in the faint red light and watched the photograph reappear in the developing tray and I had her move it through the other baths, and when she attached it to the line, she stepped back to consider the print, her shoulder pressed against my chest.

"Voilà," I said, to say something. "Magic."

Anna was silent and then took a step forward, leaning over the photograph and separating us.

"Still a little too dark. I want this last flare of light in the sky. Not so much dark clouds."

"They give some definition."

"I don't care. I want more light."

"Okay."

She placed another blank sheet of paper on the easel. When she looked back over her shoulder her already dark lips were blood-red in the light.

"Thank you for teaching me this."

Again, a little too much.

"I'm just giving you more work, really. You're now our darkroom tech."

I remember she stepped close in the darkness and the silence, and I felt her hands just above my wrists, giving them a quick, soft, but somehow violent squeeze. I was briefly aware of her face so near mine the rest of the tiny room disappeared, and then she stepped back and I had a silhouetted view of her small, trim figure, the tangle of her hair lit with fire. The warmth of her hands lingered, seemed to move up my body.

"No, Eric, I love it," she said. "I love how you can change things."

When did this take place? Was it before or after the night of the carnival? I think it must have been before. Art and Louise on the sidewalk, Anna's minute hesitation, her uncomfortableness with lying, would I have noticed any of that in the days immediately after my father died? I don't think so. I think it must have been shortly before, a memory that still sparks with half-formed images of what might have been.

But I choose to place it here, to escape briefly the night of that two a.m. telephone call, when I would drive half drunk across the state, sobering up in time to stand outside my childhood home at dawn, afraid to enter, knowing there was nothing I could do to make anything better. The worst part of my year in Shannon was ahead of me that morning.

"—I love how you can change things," she said.

"Sure," I said, and I didn't really understand, but today I have a lifetime of memories hanging on the line, all fixed and too late to shade with anything but lies, and of course I do. It would be a long time before the flattened horizon held the possibility of a new day. So forgive me if I move my hand gently across the page and place this scene here—Anna and I, alone in the darkroom, burning light into a dying sky.

Chapter 15

I WENT HOME FOR A WEEK. The funeral was the fourth day and I spent a couple of days helping my mother sort through my father's papers and watching my brother and sister suffer without any idea what to do about it. On the sixth day the bell rang and my mother came back with a curious look to tell me there was someone at the door for me.

Emily was standing on the steps in a black dress and black stockings, a formal look undone only slightly by the scuffed black Converses she was wearing. Her sun-streaked hair had grown longer and more confused since I had last seen her. Her eyes were the same startling blue but rimmed by exhaustion and her skin looked oddly pale and uneven for midsummer. She was holding a card nervously in front of her like a child not sure she was welcome at a party.

Since the moment I had arrived home to find that my father was truly and forever dead, my mood had alternated between a blank, all-encompassing sense of loss and a strange gallows humor that seemed to be the only way I could feel anything.

"This is your idea of mourning wear?" I said, discovering I had swung again toward the existentially comic point of view.

"I didn't know what to wear." She looked down at her clothes, sounding more scared and uncertain than I could remember. "I'm sorry."

"That's okay. We're going to have a black-tennis-shoe wake later on. You'll fit right in."

"I mean, I'm sorry about your father. Terry told me yesterday. I'm sorry I missed the funeral. I would've come."

I was still standing in the doorway. She'd never met my father. I had told her about his stroke. I couldn't remember what else I'd told her, but it wasn't that much and it was very strange to see her here, standing on my mother's step, waiting to be let in.

"How are you?" Emily asked nervously.

I opened my mouth and discovered my mood had oscillated back. I shook my head in a way that could mean anything, but really meant: *I can't speak*.

"How are you?" I asked.

"Oh, you know. Not so great."

I stepped out of the house and Emily followed me. My family lived in a quiet neighborhood of old Victorian houses not far from the university. It was a still day, the sky a formal Spode-blue, the street so hushed every house we passed felt as if it were listening in.

"You're still in school?"

"Not really."

"And you're still with . . ." I couldn't remember his name.

"Not really."

"What happened?"

"He got me sick."

I stopped to look at her. She shook her head impatiently and thrust the card into my hands.

"It doesn't matter. I brought this for you."

It didn't matter. We continued walking. This street was where I had grown up and it was all strange: every window, every door, every glint of light on every mailbox was familiar and so alien I felt I had tumbled into a badly made movie set.

"How do you like that little town, Sharon, you're living in?"

"Shannon. It's fine."

"I thought I might come out and visit you sometime."

"It's a long drive."

"Not so long. Just an interstate. No traffic."

"I live above the bank," I said.

We came to the end of the block and it was time to turn around or take a much longer walk.

"I'm sorry, Ricky," Emily said. "I really am."

She turned and ran back down the street to her car, the last unexploded Ford Pinto in the universe. She had an awkward girlish gait, all knees and flying elbows, that made her seem younger than she was, and she was young. We were young. I remember, and I feel our youth like an ancient memory of lightness in the bones.

. . .

I HADN'T TOLD ANYONE at the *Sentinel* my father had died. I'd meant to, but when I left a message on Art's office phone I couldn't say the words. I only told him I had a family emergency and had to go home for a while. But when I came back they all knew. The obituary had run in several newspapers and maybe they found out that way. I never asked. I walked into the office on my first morning back and Edith was standing at the counter, editing a notice by firmly crossing out words with a blunt pencil. She set it down when I came through the door.

"Sorry to hear your news, kiddo."

I nodded.

"We would have come for the funeral if we'd known," she said with a hint of reproach.

"It's a long way to go."

"Not so long for a friend," Edith said. "We would have come if we'd known."

And, unexpectedly, I had come home. I nodded again, unable to trust my voice. The front office was deserted except for Edith.

"Where's Anna?"

"She's been feeling ill." Edith picked up her pencil and crossed out an entire line without hesitation. "Headaches again."

Anna almost always *looked* healthy. She was one of those people who move with a gentle precision that makes you think all is well. Only the tiredness that sometimes puffed the skin around her eyes gave her away. Yet in the time I knew her, she was ill more than she was well. It took me a long time to realize this because she rarely missed work, usually when one of her children was sick. But her body was where all the damage in her life claimed its toll. She had headaches. She had problems with her sinuses that would finally require surgery, and the arthritis, so bad sometimes I would see her wince as she reached for her ever-present coffee cup.

None of this I understood then. None of this I took into consideration when I asked her to stay late, to take on a little extra work, none of this registered when I noticed with mild impatience how she seemed unable to get started some mornings. I see her at her desk, and one hand is extended and frozen in a half fist on the cold metal surface, and she is so still, so still, and I see now this was a struggle with pain. A crease appears above her closed eyes and I know. I hear the hesitation in the middle of a sentence and I understand. The only part of the wisdom that supposedly comes with age that I've found has any real value is learning to recognize other people's pain. But standing at the counter as a young man whose father had just died I was too lost in my own loss, which existed in my mind as a vast and featureless plain, a Bonneville Salt Flats of the soul, with the sun glinting hard off the crystalline remains of the dead sea, to understand Anna's absence.

"I left you with one of the biggest issues of the year, the anniversary issue," I said, abstractly seeing how I had let them down. "How did you get the paper out?"

"Oh, Anna's been in until today. Working with Louise." Edith finished with the notice by penciling in a final apostrophe. "You might have a headache, too."

I sat down at my desk. There was no one else in the office at this hour, just a day after the paper had been out. I really had nothing to do. After a few minutes, I stood up and walked outside. Edith raised an eyebrow as I passed, but went back to work without saying anything.

Todd was strolling across the street, yawning. He stopped when he saw me and covered his mouth awkwardly.

"Sorry, need coffee. Man, I'm sorry about your dad."

"Thanks."

"No, I mean . . ." He shook his head, considered me with sad, bewildered eyes, and then looked down the street. "You wanna, I don't know, get a beer tonight or anything? Or maybe just hang out. Watch the game."

"Yeah, I don't know. Maybe."

"All right. Anyway, hey . . ."

"Yeah. Thanks."

I was a ways farther down the sidewalk when Todd shouted after me.

"Hey, I got you a card!"

He was still standing in the doorway, his lanky frame outlined in the morning reflection on the glass door.

"You got me a card?" It was strange to hear my own voice sound so foreign, so uncertain and thin.

"Yeah. I sent it to your family's. I didn't know when you'd be back." He shrugged.

"Okay. Thank you. *Thanks.*"

"Naah, it's nothing. See you later, right?"

He waved and opened the door. A card. The tyranny of the greeting card industry and its reduction of every genuine emotion to a sub-five-dollar commodity had long been something I hated, even at twenty. And now this. A card. I squeezed my eyes shut to stop the tears.

I walked to the door that led to my apartment but realized I didn't want to go up. I walked on down Main Street until I came to the railroad tracks. I stood there while the red light started to blink and the crossing guards came down. The train announced itself with a swelling thunder that shook the ground beneath my feet before it trundled into view, the engineer visible on high as a severe figure through a smeared gray window, then an endless succession of coal cars, slowly accelerating until they became a blur, a wall. The world divided and severed.

I turned and walked back to the office. Anna was sitting at her desk when I returned. She looked up and I could tell she had watched me coming down the sidewalk. My father had been dead for a week but I was already numb to the look of condolence that greets you when you see people the first time, the combination of sympathy and awkward uncertainty, the wish they weren't facing this moment, the sense of inadequacy that left them feeling somewhat ashamed and hurried to get it over. Beneath all that was something else, a buried but inescapable sense of distance that came from the idea that they were still safely on the other side of a chasm. They stood in the land of the living, taking refuge in the idea they had permanent residence.

Anna swiveled her chair slightly to face me as I came around the counter, and this is one of those times I can see her so clearly. She was wearing dark slacks, a brown vest, and a long-sleeve white shirt, leaving her, as always, overdressed for the summer weather, but lending a kind of formality to her appearance. She did not stand. She didn't say a word. Her dark brown eyes, almost obsidian in the day and always bottomless in the way they held light, watched me, and her look was one of stark, immediate pain. It enveloped me as I sat down at my desk and seemed the first true comprehension of where I had arrived. My own grief felt cradled and suffused in a larger sea of loss. Of course, I thought, it comes to us all in time. And there was something else in Anna's look, a final acknowledgment. *Welcome.*

Chapter 16

SHANNON WAS BEAUTIFUL THAT SUMMER. I had lived there for months and never seen it as anything more than another gray prairie town, half blown away and barely there. But it was beautiful, leafy and gentle on somnolent streets where old houses stood in islands of shade even at noon. A furtive restlessness lived beneath the torpor of the long, hot days, as if people could feel the season passing too fast. Even the trains that rumbled through town seemed filled with a blood-rush of motion, an artery flowing into the body of the nation while Shannon beat on steadily at its heart.

I went back to see my family every weekend for the first month, but as I drove into Shannon on State Highway 18, the mirrored windows at the very top of the grain silos towering above the town welcomed me back with an understanding gaze. Home. I had come home.

Todd kept inviting me over for a Twins game or a game of pool at the Buffalo, but I knew he'd rather be spending time with Christine. Art and Louise took me out to lunch and people kept stopping by our table to say they were sorry. Everyone knows everything in a small town. Paul Strand and his wife had me over for dinner and I realized his oldest boy was the starting guard on the high school basketball team.

I suppose I did my job. I don't remember. I remember working with Anna in the back shop on Thursdays and that she filled my silences by talking more than she had. I learned about her early fascination with Nancy Drew, not because of the mysteries, which were easy even for an eight-year-old to figure out, but because of the blue roadster, the distant, successful father (her own parents almost never left the farm), and the repeated tropes: the endless secret passages, how Nancy or one of her friends was forever giving their location away by stepping on a loudly snapping twig, how the threat of violence never turned into violence, and Nancy's voice remained confident and smart through book after book. I learned about her later love of Edna St. Vincent Millay and Frost. She spoke of reading at night in the wilds of North Dakota, reading until she saw the light changing over the broken, blank land, with a distant smile, as if she could not quite believe she had been that girl. I remember being aware those long summer nights we worked together how beautiful she was, how she was part of the beauty of this place at this time. But all my emotions seemed to arrive from a distance, barely an echo of real feeling, and I felt her beauty not as a focus of desire, but as a balm, an object of healing contemplation, a quiet grace.

Often I was hardly there. We stepped out onto the street after a Thursday night and Anna's car was parked in the direction of the bank, so we strolled down the sidewalk together. I had gotten a call from my mother earlier in the day and I'd had a hard time concentrating on work. My brother was having trouble at school and my mother wanted me to come home and talk to him. I had nothing to say to him except, "Stop screwing around at school," which seemed unlikely to make a difference. He had never listened to me. I was not his father.

So it had been a hard night and at some point I had flat-lined, not getting much done and saying less. Anna had worked silently beside me as she walked beside me now.

"My wrists," she said.

I stopped, pulled abruptly out of myself.

"They're rope burns."

It took a moment to understand all she was telling me, and then part of my mind recoiled.

"They wouldn't leave a scar like that. Not forever."

"They do if you tear away the scabs."

"Why would you do that?"

"To remember."

We were standing by the window of the insurance office next to the bank and I realized we had walked a block past her car.

"It was a time of not thinking clearly," she said. "You remember anyway."

The streetlight reflected off the plate glass and Anna was a photogravure in its black-mirror surface, the dark pools of her eyes and the cupped line of her upturned chin a double image of the face turned toward me, and this was one of those times when she was just too beautiful.

"And now I have to wear long sleeves."

I shook my head, not wanting to hear this, having trouble focusing.

"But . . . what . . ."

Her perfect stillness told me there would be no answer.

"What did you tell your kids? They must have seen them."

"I told them I had an accident. I caught my sleeves on fire over the stove."

"Really? They believed that?"

"Oh, Eric, when you have kids you'll see—they want to believe what you tell them, especially about something that scares them. They'll figure out it doesn't make any sense when they're older, but . . . " Anna looked at her half-revealed self in the glass. "It felt necessary, but it was stupid. Don't do it. Don't make it worse than it is by punishing yourself. You have so *much* going for you . . ." She paused awkwardly, embarrassed, and shook her head impatiently. "Just let everything heal. Don't make it into a badge. Don't pretend it's not there, but don't hold on to it, okay?"

It was one of the longer declarations I'd heard her make.

"That's a lot of *don'ts*," I said.

She smiled, and the woman in the mirror smiled in a darker reflection.

"All my life lessons are don'ts."

"This is the worst thing that happened to you," I said. "You told me because it's the worst thing that happened to you."

She closed her eyes and I saw with horror that it wasn't.

"I'm okay," I said.

"Sure you are. You're twenty years old. How could you be anything else?"

"I am," I insisted. "I'm sorry I was so out of it tonight."

"You were fine. The paper's out. Go home and go to bed."

In the glass her hand rose in a stark line. I felt it appear as a living thing as she gently squeezed my arm. Anna. It was a mystery to me how I had ended up standing on this street listening to her. This woman who had become my closest friend.

. . .

I OPENED MY APARTMENT DOOR and knew someone was inside as soon I stepped into the hall. I walked as silently as possible into the living room. Emily sat slumped in the chair by the window, pushed just far enough back she was invisible from the street.

"You should lock your door."

"No one locks their door here."

I turned on the light.

"Well, look what can happen." She smiled weakly. "An intruder."

Chapter 17

A WOMAN CHECKS INTO A CHEAP MOTEL; it sounds like the start of a tasteless joke. She sits on the edge of the bed. Has she brought the bleach with her, wrapped in a brown paper bag like some cheap whiskey, or does she discover it somewhere in the room, perhaps left beneath the bathroom sink by an inattentive housecleaner? Does seeing the bottle crystallize the vision that brought her here, or is the scene already formed—the room, the bed, the bottle, darkness, peace—simply waiting to be realized?

A woman sits on the edge of a motel room bed. She holds a one-quart white plastic bottle in her hands, perhaps the most banal vessel in a world filled with the cheap and disposable. Does this strike her? Does she think about this or about anything? How long does she sit there? Are there regrets or is this moment beyond regret? Is this moment already its own conclusion?

All these questions take refuge in false abstraction. This is not "a woman." This is Anna, who had as keen an eye for beauty as anyone I have known. How could she have escaped the absurdity, the self-negating plainness of the instrument she had chosen to end her life? This is Anna, whose attention to the world around her so often seemed to come with a wistfulness at the perpetual disappearance of the now. How could she not have regret? How long does she hesitate on that bed? How close does she come to setting the bottle down, to walking back out the door?

I turn these questions over and over to find a different answer every time.

. . .

THE WHEAT FIELDS RIPENED, the sunflowers flowered, and the prairie grass dried and burned, the land turning various shades of brown and gold, even as the sky still reflected a perfect Mediterranean blue a thousand miles from the sea. Shannon merchants held their *August Crazy Day Sales!* and we ran an extra section to herald the event and reap our own harvest of advertising. Anna and I were working on the layout early in the evening when we realized we had a problem. We were half a page short, even running all the filler we had in reserve.

"We could run a house ad," Anna suggested.

"It'll look like shit," I said. I was tired and couldn't think and didn't really care. "This is a publisher's decision. Let me talk to Art."

"He's out of town. He left yesterday."

August was the time of vacations, so I don't know why this felt wrong.

"Art and Louise left town?"

"Just Art."

"Really?"

Earlier in the evening Anna had tried to lighten the mood, reading me the social notes from the women's auxiliary of the local Moose Club, which involved a break-dancing contest for women over fifty. I knew in some abstract sense it was sweet and I should respond, but I couldn't. My desolation was like an electric field filling the room. For the last hour we had worked in silence.

"I think Art needed a getaway," she said, her eyes too carefully focused on the notes she was scribbling on a design sheet.

"But Louise is here?"

"Yes."

"I'll talk to her."

"I can do it."

For some reason that irritated me.

"I'm the editor," I said. "I'll take care of it."

I walked across the street to the Shoemakers' small square one-story house, right next to the one Todd rented from them. I had never been inside, and when I came to the door, I knocked, waited, knocked again, and then cracked open the door.

"Louise?"

I heard a noise like a rustling of paper or the scurrying of mice and then a sound, not quite a word.

"It's me, Eric. Can I come in?"

Her voice was again indistinct, but I thought I heard yes.

The door opened into a narrow kitchen with yellowed linoleum, once-white cabinets, an antiquated refrigerator the same faded color humming nervously in the corner. A doorway without a door waited on the opposite wall. I stepped through it into a forest.

A forest in the gloaming, thick white trunks crowding around me, oddly rough and squarish. My eyes adjusted and I was looking at stacks of newspapers, stack after stack piled toward the ceiling in a man-made glade, kept in perpetual dusk by pulled drapes. There was just enough room to move between them. I could make out what I thought was the corner of a couch on the far side of the room, but I couldn't see anyone.

"Louise?"

"Ricky."

I slid sideways between the paper towers, afraid what would happen if I knocked one over. I pictured both of us swimming for our lives in a bone-dry sea. Louise was sitting on the floor, her back against the wall, her knees up, her toes under the side of the couch. A handful of newspaper pages rested in her lap, propped up so they fell in a sliver of fading light escaping around the drapes. Beside her hip a paper cup stood next to a square-shouldered bottle of Old Grand-Dad. There was something tidy and domestic about the placement of the glass and the bottle, as if their positions had been methodically worked out over time.

"We've been meaning to clean up," Louise said. "Sorry about the mess."

I had forgotten why I'd come.

"Take a seat. Tell me you're having fun."

I sat down on the couch, and it was when she looked directly at me, and I saw that the solar furnace of her eye had gone out, that I truly felt the wrongness of it all.

"Are you okay?" I said. "Why are you sitting on the floor?"

"It's comfortable. I don't like . . ." She tilted her head, indicating something about the world above floor level that met with her disapproval. Her words were slightly slowed and slurred.

"There's a problem with the layout," I said, remembering. "Swanson's is pulling its ad."

"I'm sorry we don't pay you more, Ricky. We don't really make any money off the paper, you know. We'd like to pay everyone more."

"It's okay," I said. It wasn't, but I had never seen her like this and I heard something small moving in a corner of the room, scratching or gnawing. I wanted to get done and get out. "The thing is, without it, we don't have enough pages for the second section."

Louise took a drink from the paper cup, setting it back in its exact spot without looking.

"What kind of newspaper depends on a weekly ad from a funeral home, anyway?" she said. "What kind of business plan is that?"

The room was too warm and had the dry, dead air of a space shut up for too long. How did they live like this? I thought about how much time Art spent in the office and how often Louise was absent, presumably here. Were these her stacks? Was she hoping to read all this someday? Why? *To keep up*, I could hear her saying. *I want to keep up*. A sense of the hidden landscapes that unfold into the infinite distance inside our heads, the towers gleaming on the horizon—tomorrow I will reach my destination, tomorrow it will be different, tomorrow I will accomplish amazing things—filled me with impatience. *You'll never get to it*, I wanted to say. *You will never,* ever *get to it and then you will run out of time.*

"I don't know," I said, "but we planned the second section for the Crazy Days sales."

"*Crazy Days*, Ricky, can you believe that? We live in crazy days."

"Crazy days, Louise. But right now we're a half page short of craziness."

"Why is Swanson [she slurred his name, *Ssshwansson*] pulling the ad?"

"Well . . ." I had just learned this from Anna a half hour earlier. "I guess we referred to a 'dressed-up corpse' being on display in an obit last week."

She cocked her head to look at me.

"We did?"

"It came in from the family late and Edith was out. I don't think anyone really looked at it."

Louise's laugh was like the rustling in the paper forest, only louder. "*Dressed-up corpse*. He does love his rouge, that sad little man."

"It's my fault," I said, trying to hurry things along. She shook her head abruptly. "Anyway," I said. "I know he's a friend of Art's, and I wondered if maybe he could talk to him. We could run a correction or something . . ."

"Art is on a trip with a friend," Louise said, finishing the drink in the paper cup and letting it fall from her hand. I watched it bounce once and roll behind a stack of papers.

"And that friend isn't Swanson," she said. "That's what this is about. He doesn't read the damn obits. He doesn't read anything. He's just jealous."

I sat on the couch. She sat in her corner on the floor. The light escaping the drapes was a narrow silver-blue bar that missed the papers in her lap and danced like a mocking sprite on her knees. I understood something. My mind swam through a small sea of confusion, but then I saw it: the way Art sometimes squeezed Todd's arm, his hand lingering a little too long; the intensity of the friendships I had noticed with a couple of older men much like himself, the strange sense of ceremony and suppressed excitement when they appeared in the office, and the way the rest of the staff tended studiously to their desks at those moments. I thought about him and Louise, the way they moved down the street, everywhere, really, the small but respectful distance they kept between the two of them, as if they had learned this was the degree of closeness that worked. I thought about how much they depended on each other at the paper, two halves of a whole, and I felt another moment of confusion and then sadness. The world is better this way now, vastly better, but then, in the small-town Midwest, it was all a matter of quiet desperation and discreet disappearance. Art was on a trip with a friend.

The silence had grown too long between us.

"We really need the ad," I said. "I could call him and say we'll run a correction . . ." I stumbled to a halt trying to imagine what that correction would be. The corpse of Henry Abbott on display at Swanson Funeral Home last Friday was *not* dressed up?

"No, you're the *editor*," Louise said. "You're not supposed to have to deal with ads. That's the publisher's job." She stood by sliding her back up against the wall. It was an impressive sight, like watching a mountain rise out of the earth. "I'll talk to the little faggot," she said, her eye flaring back into a fierce, tumbling solar cauldron. "You'll get the ad back."

I walked across the street in the early evening silence.

"Art's out of town," I said when I got back to the office.

"I know," Anna said. "I told you."

"Louise is going to deal with it."

"Okay . . ."

"Just hold the space for now. The ad will come back in."

She nodded and returned to work.

"Art's out of town with a friend," I said.

"I know, Eric."

I looked around for something to do and then gave up, leaning against the wheel of the old letterpress.

"Does everybody but me know that Art goes out of town with friends?"

Anna smiled ever so slightly. "I'm not so sure Sam knows," she said, referring to her ten-year-old daughter.

I watched Anna use a ruler to sketch out the design of a page.

"I'm the editor," I said. "I'm supposed to know stuff."

"You know lots of stuff, Eric. It's okay you didn't know this. What does it really matter, anyway?"

I went over to the other light table, where I had a couple of half-finished layouts, and pretended to work. The radio was playing a Kris Kristofferson song, something about drinking too much. It didn't matter, but then, nothing felt like it did.

"I just don't like not noticing."

"They've been here forever, you know," Anna said. "They knew each other in grade school, high school. I think he was the best friend she ever had. They got married when she came back to town after getting fired at the *Fargo Forum*."

I understood what she was trying to tell me, but I didn't know what to say.

"I didn't know she got fired."

"She pissed off the biggest business in town, the sugar beet processing plant. The story won an award, but the *Fargo Forum* really wasn't about challenging the business community."

"What did she write?"

"A story about how much the plant stunk."

I laughed.

"He took her in," Anna said. "A job first, but they ended up together."

"Okay."

We worked quietly for a bit.

"Still . . ." I said.

She stopped working and turned, a mixture of impatience and sympathy on her face.

"Still, what?"

"Still, wouldn't you want it to be, you know . . . I mean, why would you want to give up . . . *sex*, and, okay, not just that—and love, too. I mean wouldn't you want everything? All the things you're supposed to have when you're together and . . ."

"I don't know that they don't love each other. And for that matter, I don't know that they've given up sex."

"Oh, Jesus—"

“It’s between them,” she said, with an edge I hadn’t heard before. I had disappointed her. “The choices they’ve made.”

I thought that was true, but part of me still wanted to protest. I had been thinking in a bewildered way about what love meant since Emily had crawled back into my bed, and I clung to a romantic ideal.

“But you don’t know that they really do, either. I mean, love each other.”

Anna shook her head and turned back to her table. “I suppose not.”

We worked in silence for a while, Anna pulling a full-sized page sheet out and beginning to fill it with waxed copy. I did the same.

“I just meant nobody really knows what anybody’s feeling.”

“I know what you meant, Eric.”

“Okay.”

“Maybe it’s enough,” Anna said. “Maybe it works for them. That’s all I was trying to say.”

• • •

TWO DAYS LATER we had a fire. It was set on purpose by the volunteer fire department so they could get in some practice, and no living thing was supposed to be at risk. The building the fire department decided to burn down was a small, abandoned grain elevator. Grain elevators are always a fire hazard because of the explosively flammable grain dust that ends up in every nook and cranny. Setting fire to an old grain elevator and putting it out seemed like good practice for what would be a serious danger should it occur.

The fire truck was parked nearby, hoses properly unrolled and positioned. The men in their heavy yellow-and-black fire-retardant suits circled the building. I joined them, notebook in hand. Anna climbed into a nearby barn to get a better angle for photos. The blaze was set and the flames were allowed to work their way up the sides of the elevator.

Except they didn't *work*, they *raced*. In a few minutes the Shannon Volunteer Fire Department surrounded a towering Roman candle. Flames reached high into the clouded sky, blown sideways by a breeze that seemed slight on the ground, but was clearly stronger at the top of the elevator, where a fountain of floating cinders, burning shards, and a thick, swirling, lovely swarm of glowing grain dust like ten million fireflies drifted through the air and onto the barn, an adjoining shed, the fire truck, and all of us.

The heat must have been intense, because the firemen fell back, the water from their hoses reaching less than halfway up the elevator. I was standing farther away and still felt it like a summer sun that had mysteriously risen twice as close to the earth.

I was backing up slowly, when the roof of the shed burst into flames and I realized Anna was still in the barn hayloft.

The barn roof must have been damp or covered with moss, because it was only smoking when I arrived, tongues of flame like the blessing of the holy spirit drifting through the smoke to land and flare briefly on the wooden shingles. Anna stood in the open door of the hayloft, camera to her eye, shooting both the elevator and the burning sky.

"Hey!" I shouted. "Time to go!"

She took another shot and lowered the camera slowly from her eye, her expression strangely serene.

"Hey, get down!"

Anna stood in the frame of the hayloft, and a curl of smoke bent out of the sky and wrapped itself around her waist. She returned the camera slowly to her eye and took another carefully framed photograph, and I suddenly felt like I didn't know her at all.

"Get down!"

She hesitated, clearly hearing me, and I thought she was about to say something. The sound of the fire behind me and the damp pop as the hot cinders landed on the roof filled the air with a low tumult of noise.

"Come on, quit fooling around."

A small flame had sprung to life on the edge of the roof, bending toward the shingles like an eager gnome. Anna's attention had returned to the river of debris and ash floating so clearly against the gray slate of the sky.

"Anna, get out of there! That's an order from your boss."

That made her smile with an odd sort of affection. She raised the camera and took another shot of the sky.

The firemen were focused on the elevator and the shed. I needed to call them over, but I couldn't take my eyes off of her, the way she was still leaning against the side of the hayloft opening. Smoke was curling out around her feet.

"Anna! Jesus! If you don't get down this second, I'm coming up there."

She looked down at me then, regretfully, and stepped back into the darkness of the hayloft. I waited a heartbeat and then I was running into the ground floor of the barn, where the darkness blinded me and I felt the smoke like a snake constricting slowly around my chest and I bumped into her as she jumped from the last step on the ladder.

We emerged into the gray light and a torrential downpour as hoses were turned on the barn, extinguishing the smoldering flames. Anna bent over double to shield the camera and we staggered out into the grass, where I sat down hard and she knelt beside me.

Paul Strand appeared in front of us, pulling his fireman's hat back in panic.

"You're both okay?"

"We're fine," Anna said. "I just waited a little too long. Sorry."

He shook his head in disbelief and returned his attention to his crew.

"Fire and ice," Anna said, coughing quietly.

"What? What the—"

"Robert Frost. 'Some say the world will end in fire. Some say in ice.'"

"Anna . . ."

"'From what I've tasted of desire I hold with those who favor fire.'"

It didn't seem she had heard me. There was a kind of euphoria in her voice.

"Awesome. Listen—"

"'I think I know enough to say that for destruction ice is also great—"

"Listen—"

"—and would suffice.' One of my favorite poems."

"*Listen*. That was stupid. That was *so* stupid. What the hell were you thinking?"

I will always remember the way she looked at me then, as if she had thought I would understand and was saddened that I didn't.

"I'm sorry," she said.

We were both soaked. I was trying to regain my composure.

"Really. What were—"

Behind me the grain elevator collapsed in on itself, the sound like a cascade of garbage tumbling down stairs. I felt a flare of heat against my back and a flock of sparks and glowing embers sailed through the air. Anna raised the camera and took a shot.

"It was just beautiful. The fire. The sky. I forgot where I was."

I was about to protest, but she had the camera back at her eye, a shield, taking pictures of the firemen now closing in to hose down the tumbled remains of the elevator. She stood and drifted closer for a final shot.

I looked up the poem in my *Norton Anthology* that night. Sitting in my apartment above the bank, I reread it several times, picturing Anna memorizing the lines as a young girl out there in the badlands, where the country itself can catch fire. As I read it seemed an odder and odder choice as anyone's favorite poem. No road not taken. No woods lovely dark and deep. No promises to keep. No hope. Fire or ice. The end, either way.

She hadn't quoted it perfectly. There had been a single omission. The actual line is, "I have known enough *of hate* to say that for destruction ice is also great."

I didn't know what to make of that, thought it was a curious mistake, and the whole event still bugged me enough that I brought it up with her at the end of the next day. We were both working late, finishing our copy. She handed me the cutlines for her photos of the fire, which were excellent, and I said:

"You misquoted Robert Frost."

"I don't quote him at all," Anna said. "I quote the fire chief."

"I mean last night." And I explained.

I could tell it annoyed and confused her. She reached absently for the cutlines still in my hand, as if they now needed a rewrite.

"I like my version better," she said.

I moved the page just out of her reach. "You're thinking of misquoting the fire chief, too?"

She realized what she was doing and pulled her hand back. "No, I think he expresses himself perfectly: 'The success of our initial efforts to ignite a conflagration exceeded our expectations.'"

"There you are," I said. "Let's see Robert Frost beat that."

We were alone in the front office, although I could hear Todd knocking around in the back shop. Anna turned to her desk, and an unexpected sense of sadness, of uncertainty, swept over me, not just at her, but everything—Emily reappearing, my father's funeral, still so recent.

"No hate," I said.

"Not always," Anna said, her typewriter rattling in a long and furious salvo.

Many years later this woman, *Anna*, sits on the edge of a motel bed, a bottle of bleach in her hands, and I can say, yes, of course, it's obvious; it was always there. But she also came down from that burning barn, and who is to say one moment is truer than the other? We are taught to believe the ending is the part that matters, but it's just the point where we lift our hands, or they are taken, from the keys. She was back at her desk that next afternoon, and I can still see her proud, unbent posture. I watch her hands come down. I hear the staccato of Anna filling another page.

Chapter 18

THE FIRST TIME HE HIT HER it was raining hard, the sound like a machine gun against the tin roof of the trailer. The baby was crying. Nobody could sleep. He had come home late, fishtailing the Pontiac down the switchback dirt road until he lost it on a corner and left the car nose-down in the ditch. He was soaked when he came through the door. Sitting at the kitchen table, he asked for a glass of water, and her arms felt strangely numb and it slipped from her hand as she was bringing it to him. The glass shattered and shards bounced across the yellow linoleum floor, and when he stood he stepped on one, cutting his foot badly, and it was only then that she noticed he was barefoot, that somewhere in the night he had lost both his boots and his socks.

He shouted in pain and swung wildly with a half-closed fist, which flashed an odd blue in the corner of her vision, and then she was sitting on the floor, staring at pieces of glass between her legs, each with a small halo of light, like gems of some incalculable value.

Before he stumbled through the door she had been lying in bed with the baby beside her, hoping that would stop the crying, listening to the mad pummel of the rain, and it had felt to her she could feel the drops falling all the way from the farthest stars to her roof, that she could apprehend the depth of the universe in the silver line of their descent. And as she rode the distance toward the small square box of her home, visible like a metal bull's-eye amid the wild country, she could trace the path of her marriage in their plummet.

The sound they made as they annihilated themselves against the corrugated tin was a shot and a hollow echo, as if the metal were snapping back into place; after a while it transformed itself into two words repeated a thousand times a minute, *too young too young too young too young too young*. Her husband was too young to be asked to come home every night and sit in the middle of nowhere with nothing to do but stare at a video or listen to the wind sneak past the cheap window frames with the squeak of nervous mice. He would try, sometimes for three or four nights in a row, but the other men were all single and they were all going into town and why shouldn't he join them for a quick drink? What could be wrong with joining them for a couple of drinks or maybe one more after that? He worked hard. He was working hard to support her and the baby and hadn't he earned a drink or two? Could she say he hadn't earned a drink or two, and if he was still the boy who had first leaned forward in the light of the dash to reveal a smile so perfect it flashed a semaphore of longing directly into her heart, and if he still had the same tangle of dirty blond hair and the same thin hard body that stretched his T-shirt and her erotic imagination, how could she blame him if these things still worked with other girls, not that much older than her, in the bars? She slid down this long straight line of reasoning through the darkness until she hit the unyielding end and felt herself dissolved in the cacophony of the rain.

Now, sitting on the floor with pieces of glass glowing like half-born angels and the air ringing like a bell, she said, "I'm sorry." And that was the wrong thing to say. She saw something change in his eyes, some shift from defeat and shame to contempt. She had made herself the one to blame and she could feel his confused heart seizing at this. She wanted to say, *I know you are not bad, I know you are not a bad man*, but maybe that was no longer true, because he grabbed her by her hair and pulled her to her feet. Bring another glass into the bedroom, he said.

And she stood there unsteadily with the world glowing and somewhere very far away the baby was still crying. How do I know this? She told me most of it later that year, and the rest I have taken a lifetime to learn. Call it fiction, if you wish, a writer filling in the blanks. But time explains things, and this is the girl who still lived in the woman I knew.

• • •

EMILY CAME AND WENT at odd times. I never knew when she would be waiting inside my apartment, ready to stay the night or for a few days, and she would only tell me she was leaving an hour at most before she was back out the door. Twice I returned at the end of the day to find a note taped to the window and a hollowness in the air where she had so recently been.

Taping the note to the glass baffled me. Why not the

counter, the bedside table? It was as if she thought the first thing I did upon returning home was march to the window to stare out at the town. I wondered how many hours a day she spent there while I was working. I knew she went out into the countryside sometimes for long drives. She would tell me about some abandoned barn or perfect country church she had discovered amid the ripening wheat fields and browning prairie grass. I asked her a few times if she wanted to go to the Buffalo Bar or have dinner at the café, but she made awkward excuses. The window was all the view of Shannon she wanted. She didn't want to meet anyone. She didn't want to have to make conversation. She didn't want to talk about the past year. She didn't want to explain. She just wanted to be there in my apartment, my living room, my bed, with nothing said, her skinny arms with their knobby elbows wrapped too tightly around my chest, her skinny leg draped over me, all with a confused fierceness that led to dreams of being entangled in hammocks, collapsed sails, or force fields cast by spectral blue-skinned aliens watching from the shadows.

Even then, even as a young man, I was the kind of person who liked to know where he stood, and it would have been intolerable to me earlier—it *had* been intolerable to me, finally, in college, the hollowness of our hold on each other—but now I couldn't seem to care. I drifted through the summer with a sense of being half awake, sliding in and out of the lassitude that hangs on the edge of a dream during a restless night. The odd thing was, after a lifetime of insomnia, I had no sense of lying awake at night. But then, I had very little sense of being awake during the day.

We did drive out into the country together at least one Sunday afternoon. I remember that the state's senior U.S. senator had come through Shannon for a ceremony marking the tenth anniversary of the bomb factory, and I'd had a chance to interview him at the end. He was a very old man, a shambling wreck with badly blotched skin and wisps of hair standing up like wind-whipped snow, but still tall, broad-shouldered, a former college football star who had once blocked for Bronko Nagurski. He only wanted to talk about the local high school teams. "You played the game, Dick?" he'd asked, and when I'd confessed that I hadn't, a light had gone out of his eyes.

I told Emily the story as we drove past a threadbare farm tucked in a grove of trees. I finished with the senator calling me "Dick," and waited.

"He was the mayor?" she asked, staring out the window.

"A senator."

"That must have been nice for you, Ricky."

"No, it was . . . " But it was too much trouble to start over.

Emily nodded, as if I had explained. Her feet were up on the dash—she never seemed to know what to do with her limbs—and she was slumped so her chin was just above the bottom of her window. She told me once her mother took all the soft pillows out of the couches and chairs in their house to make sure she sat up straight as a little girl, and she'd decided then she'd never sit with her two feet on the floor and her hands in her lap again. It was one of the few things I knew about her childhood, except that her family had a lot of money; her father did something in banking while her mother worked on straightening spines. Seeing the soft curve of her against the seat, my familiarity with her body, with the way she moved, how it felt to have her close at night, stole over me, and I wondered if we might have a future after all. I wanted it to be so, or I wanted to want it to be so, and they felt like the same thing to me suddenly, as if in every desire what really mattered was the buried longing for feeling itself.

Emily peered out of the car window, her eyes barely above the glass.

"The people who live out here," she said, "do you think this is where they really wanted to be, or did they just end up here?"

"I don't know. Some of them. Ranchers and farmers. People who like cows . . . or wheat."

"What do you think they do?"

"What do you mean? They work. Just like everybody."

"I mean, besides that. What do they do with the rest of the day?"

"I don't know. The same things as everybody. Watch TV, read books, have hobbies. Why, you thinking of taking up ranching?"

But Emily had stopped listening again, her eyes tracking a yellow yield sign riddled with bullet holes as we crossed another deserted country road.

Chapter 19

Art had long ago returned from his trip out of town with a friend, but he and Louise had been keeping separate hours in the office. You hardly saw them together. At first, when Art was in, I found myself watching him more closely—previously, it had always been Louise who burned up the oxygen in the room—trying to find something that would help me understand the duality of his life. But there was nothing I could see, and very soon I stopped paying attention and he was just benignly smiling, rotund, slightly nervous Art, and it was only when his office sat empty after lunch and the front office had that strangely vacant air of expectancy, as we waited for Louise to appear, that I sometimes briefly thought about it all.

The UPS man arrived with several oversized boxes late one morning. A half hour or so later, Art emerged from his office, beaming.

"Everyone," he said. "I have something I want you to see."

It was a quiet day, with only Anna, Edith, and me out front. Art stepped through the door to the back shop and repeated the invitation. Todd appeared, rubbing ink off the back of his hand and shooting me a curious look.

Art opened the door to his office and stepped to the side, as if revealing the grand prize in a game show. We all crowded in. There was a moment of silence.

"What is it?" Edith asked.

"It's a computer," Todd said, the awe clear in his voice. "An Apple II computer."

Art had relocated a large pile of papers onto the floor and cleared a space at a credenza for a collection of beige boxes: keyboard, floppy drives, and cathode ray monitor. A green cursor quietly blinked its invitation.

"A computer," Edith said, as if someone had just told her Art had purchased a solid gold canoe. "What in the world are we going to do with a computer?"

Art squeezed around us. He placed his hands carefully and gently on the keyboard, pressed a key, and columns of green numbers blinked into existence.

"You can use it to do spreadsheets," he said. "Look."

"Wow," Todd said.

"A computer," Edith said again. "I suppose we'll get a rocket ship next."

The door opened and shut out in the front office, and after a second Louise filled the doorway. She looked at the boxes on the credenza, the blinking screen.

"It's here," she said to Art, smiling slowly at him with the slightly embarrassed pride of two people who have decided on an extravagance.

He smiled back. "It is."

We shuffled over and she slid into the room by his side. She reached up and squeezed his shoulder, and for the briefest of moments he leaned in to her. "Fantastic," Louise said.

"Yeah," Todd said, "these things are going to take over. We'll all be using them someday."

Edith scoffed. "What would I ever use a computer for?"

"To type up your notices," Todd said, "and the recipes for Kitchen Korner."

"A *computer* for typing up recipes?" Edith laughed. "I hardly need an electric typewriter."

"I don't know if it'll ever replace the typewriter, but it could be useful for . . ." Louise gestured airily into the future. The cursor blinked at us. Anna and I glanced at each other. She shrugged. I look back, and the typewriters on our desks, the hulking printing press in the backroom, the hay-bale-sized rolls of newsprint stacked against the wall, were already growing fainter with every blink. But none of us, except Todd, the printer who worked in the middle of machines, could see it. My own thoughts were on Art and Louise, now leaning happily against each other, wondering why the sight of them like this filled me with such sadness.

. . .

THERE WAS THIS quiet contest among the farmers in the county to be the first to harvest a field of wheat. It struck me as faintly ridiculous, since the next guy usually started just a day or two later. But, still, in the middle of August in the middle of North Dakota, news is what it is, so Anna and I were both present as the combine took its first swath across a rippling field of burnished gold, tossing a gray-gold spray of dust into the air that meant it traveled in its own small cloud.

I had already interviewed the farmer, a young guy with a barely there mustache. I watched Anna, crouched in the wheat stubble, shoot a few shots of the combine heading down the field before she trudged back to join me by my car.

"I need another pass when he comes back, I think," she said.

I nodded. We leaned against the fender of the Camaro and watched the combine sailing down the flat gold sea. North Dakota's fields all seemed to run right off the edge of the earth. The fields in my part of Minnesota were held closer, bound by lines of trees, creeks or small lakes, ragged at the edges, the original wild country holding its contours despite generations of human effort to subdue it. My father liked to take Sunday drives and we were always piling into the car and rambling down state highways through this country. I remembered the way he slowed down when we came to an unexpected glade of trees tangled around a creek or when a windbreak of pines parted to reveal the glinting scimitar of a pond in the late light.

He loved the fall; it was his favorite season, and, leaning against the car with Anna, I was suddenly taken with a memory of wandering out into a field much like the one before us, shaved wheat stubble scraping our ankles as we tried to get a better look at a pile of white stones some farmer had arranged in the shape of a miniature castle.

The sun had been falling just like this and the field had the same ripe smell of grain dust and black earth. My father stopped, my mother beside him, not wanting to get too close and spoil the illusion, not wanting to see the imperfections that would inevitably be revealed in this small homemade creation. The smile they shared as they stood together, a smile I noticed only barely then—before all three of their kids whooped down the field to get a better look at the castle—but now could see so clearly, seemed the center of that half-forgotten day.

I had to look away from the field being combined. It was suddenly too bright and gold.

"Your husband. What was he like?"

Anna had been watching something move across the sky. A hawk. Her face didn't turn my way but I saw her eyes lose their focus.

"Really. I know it didn't work out. But there must have been something. At first."

"I am done—"

"*With men*. I know. But, really, at the beginning."

"Eric."

"I know. I just. I mean, there must have been something."

"I was young," Anna said. "Too young to know better."

The hawk was in a long glide toward a corner of the field, where it dropped the last few feet in a wings-arrested plummet.

"Poor mouse," Anna said.

"I know it was a mistake," I said. "I know he was . . . not nice—"

She laughed the way you laugh when something is very much not funny.

"Okay," I said, "but my father used to drive my mother crazy with these things he would do. He traded away her car one time without asking her because he was sure she'd love a Volkswagen beetle, but she hated driving a manual transmission. She didn't really have her own car after that. He spent half their savings once on this crazy modern sculpture he thought she'd love. Sometimes when I was a kid, I didn't understand why they were even together, but then there'd be these other moments. I was watching Art and Louise today and I just . . . "

Anna kept her attention on the field, camera at the ready. But she was blinking rapidly and, when she stole a glance at me, I could see something in my question was harder for her than I understood.

"I don't know, Eric. It wasn't anything like that for me. I don't know. But people aren't perfect, you know. People aren't perfect. But some are worse."

At the far end of the field the combine had turned a corner and was headed back our way. It looked more than ever like a squat green galleon sailing through the windswept grain. I didn't even know what I was trying to ask, or why it felt so important.

"Okay," I said. "Yeah."

Anna stared blankly into the sky.

"He came from the South. He had a drawl. And a *way*. A Southern way, cocky and shy at the same time. This kind of smile. And these great cheekbones. I thought he knew about the world. But he didn't. That's all, Eric. I never think about him anymore. He is a blank spot in my life. He is not there."

"But you thought you loved him? I mean, at first?"

"Eric."

"Sorry. Forget it."

The combine thrummed as it approached, the sound sorting itself out into a diesel roar, the mechanical crunch of the head sweeping up the wheat stalks, and the tumult of threshed grain tumbling into the back. Anna said something I couldn't hear.

"What?"

"Nothing." Anna said. "Look at this. This is the moment." She gestured toward the machine heading our way and, as it crested a slight ridge in the field, it seemed immense, framed against the blue sky, with the distant water tower of Shannon visible off its left shoulder, a briefly perfect frame on an unexceptional subject. I hadn't been paying close enough attention.

Chapter 20

EARLY SEPTEMBER, THE KIDS BACK IN SCHOOL, the farmers deep into harvest. I was perched on an uncomfortable chair in the narrow living room of an old man who sat on a recliner covered in a corduroyish material once embossed with a British hunting scene, faded dogs and flushed birds peeking out behind his bony shoulders.

The walls were filled with shelves, and the shelves were filled with liquor bottles and small statues, and the liquor bottles and small statues were all in the shape of Elvis: Young Elvis, Hollywood Elvis, Army Elvis, Hawaii Elvis, Cowboy Elvis, Vegas Elvis, Comeback Elvis, Post-Comeback Elvis. Some were just heads. Some were Romanesque busts. Some, the full Elvisian form. Elvis wore black leather, white leather, jeans, an army uniform, a swimsuit, denim shirt, six-gun cowboy hat jumpsuit martial-arts-robe-toga-sort-of-thing. In some he held a guitar; in some he danced; in at least two he wore sunglasses. Some were porcelain. Some were glass. All were Elvis.

I held my notebook in front of me. This was our human-interest feature for the week.

"So," I said. "You must really like Elvis."

The old man nodded, his eyes unnaturally bright.

"Not really."

"Great. Wait. Not really?"

"Nope."

"Okay . . . Then why do you have all these?"

The old man was a little too thin and his hair had started to recede in a way that gave him the aspect of a slightly deranged, crested bird. He grinned cheerfully at me from the faded meadow of his recliner.

"I'm seventy-four years old," he said. "I have to do *something*."

I was back in the office, standing beside Anna's desk, telling her the story. "'I have to do *something*,'" I said, waiting for her to laugh, or at least smile, and then I was crying, staring above her head at the blurred blue-green day beyond the window and crying, tears running down my face I could feel and only Anna could see.

"I have to do something," I said again, believing I hadn't quite managed to deliver the punch line.

"It's a good story," Anna said. "What do you have to do next?"

"Nothing, really."

"Let's go out to the lake. They're having some sort of sail-boat race. I could use your help with the pictures."

. . .

THE SAILBOATS WERE ALL small training boats, their neon sails creased against the green bank on the far side of the water. We stood on the bluffs of a small island that could be reached by a bridge, and Anna shot with a long telephoto lens as they passed. The wind blew her hair across the camera and without thinking I reached up and held it back as she shot.

"Thank you," she said, after a brief but visible stiffness in her shoulders.

She lowered the camera from her eyes.

"I think that's enough from here."

The short ride out to the lake had been silent. I'd brushed the tears away before turning to face the office, but in the car I could still feel their dried tracks stitched down my cheeks like threads holding me together.

"Maybe a few more down by the dock as they come in," Anna said, staring at the dam that ran like a gray chalk line at the north side of the lake. "But that won't be for a while."

I nodded. She didn't need my help at all, really. There was only one camera and she had the better eye. We sat down on a bench a few feet from the edge of the bluff and let the sky envelop us. Everything below us was fake, the lake, the island, which had been made by dredging a channel to cut off a promontory, even the beach to the right, sand dragged in from some gravel pit. But it didn't matter, the light was soft, scattered by canvas clouds, and all the colors of the day had a gentle clarity.

"So," Anna said.

"Yeah. I don't know."

"Sure you do, Eric."

"Not really, I mean, sure. Yes. But not really. Nothing I feel seems to have anything to do with anything, with anything that's actually going on right then. I just—"

But there was no *just*, or if there was, I had no idea what it was. We watched the sailboats make an awkward shuffling turn near the dam, sails luffing, hulls bobbing as the sound of laughter and someone exhorting them to clearer action drifted up off the surface of the water.

"The guy has like ten thousand Elvis bottles," I said. "Can you think of a stupider waste of time?"

"Oh, I can. I can think of lots of worse things."

"But *Elvis*. Elvis with a lei around in his neck, wearing a white jumpsuit in a painted green ceramic bottle. I mean, that's not even historically accurate. Hawaii Elvis and Vegas Elvis are two *completely* different Elvi. You can't mix them up like that! It's just . . . *wrong*."

Anna was silent.

"Elvi?"

And I felt myself crying again, helplessly.

"I believe the *OED* lists the accepted plural form as Elvi."

"Well. The *OED*."

The sailboats were passing the island again, tacking against the wind, less organized as they angled to keep their sails taut. I could make out the figures more clearly in the shallow hulls, hunched forward as if propelling themselves into the breeze. White and blue hulls. White- and yellow- and blue- and green-striped sails. I felt like I could sit on the bench and watch them pass for the rest of my life.

I heard the camera click beside me and click again. I turned and Anna was putting it down. I had the sense she hadn't been focused on the sailboats, but me. I brushed my cheeks but the tears had blown dry.

"I collected fossils when I was a little girl," she said, "out in the hills around our farm. I collected all these little pieces I found. I told myself I was going to be a paleontologist. Go all over the world and discover new dinosaurs. I even made up names for them. The Hopasaurus. Stridasaurus Rex. *Megasaur.*"

She held her hair back against the wind, smiling as she remembered.

"You really found fossils?"

"No, they were just the bones of dead animals. Rabbits mostly, I think."

"Thus, Hopasaurus."

"Thus, Hopasaurus."

"But Megasaur?"

"Probably a buffalo. I can't really remember. But it was something big. And it was a big thing for me. I thought I might visit Africa. I thought I might wear a *pith* helmet."

"Wow."

"Yes, wow. The thing is, everybody needs their wow. Everybody needs their Elvi. I'm sorry this is a hard time, Eric. I don't know what to say to you. It just is. And it will be for a while and then it won't be quite as bad, but it won't ever go away, either." She hesitated, as if her thoughts had been diverted down a different path.

"But you think I could use a hobby."

She laughed. "Beyond quoting the *OED*, yes, I think you could use a hobby. Something to care about, or at least something to take your mind off things."

"I care about all kinds of things. I care about everything."

Anna stood and moved quickly to the edge of the bluff, shooting the boats briefly arrayed in a fan across the sparkling water, each sail like a cupped palm waving goodbye. I hadn't seen the shot at all.

"How's Emily?"

"I don't know. She comes and goes."

"Are you okay with that?"

"I don't know. Sure. No. Whatever. I don't care."

She held the camera at her chest, watching the sails disappear into the scattered light of the lake.

"You need to care, Eric. And you need to find something to do, something that takes you from this day to the next one. That's what people do. That's how they manage."

. . .

ANNA WAS IN THE DARKROOM and Edith had mysteriously disappeared into the back shop, so I was alone in the front office when Louise came through the door, sat down on the corner of my desk, and fixed me with her death-ray eye.

"I hear you had a breakdown, Ricky. I hear you were *breaking down* in the newsroom."

Perhaps it hadn't been quite as unnoticed as I'd thought.

"Uhm . . ."

"Artie and I have talked about it. We've had a *discussion*, Ricky, and we believe we've been working you too hard. You're young. You're strong. We thought you were invulnerable. We treated you like you were Superboy. Now we realize we've asked too much. You're dad *died*, Ricky, he's dead! He's *gone*!

I was not close to my own father—he was an asshole—but that must be painful. We want you to be having fun. We think you should take a week off. Take a vacation. Go to a lake. Go *fishing*."

She said this with radiant enthusiasm, as if hearts could be restarted, limbs reattached, sins undone by impaling a worm and casting it into a lake.

"I don't really like to fish," I said.

This worried her even more. "Just some time on a boat," she said, a slight edge of panic in her voice. "Get out, Ricky, enjoy the fresh air. Nature! It's *rejuvenating*. It can refresh the mind and the *soul*. We want you to take some time off! Have some *fun*!"

Louise insisted that my rejuvenating, fun vacation start immediately. I told her I was only going to take a couple of days and would be back in time to paste up the next issue. I thought I might go home to see how my mother was doing, but when I came to the interstate, I turned west, heading in the opposite direction from both my family and the healing waters of Minnesota's ten thousand lakes. I had never been to the badlands in western North Dakota except once, on a camping trip when I was very young—all I remembered was a brown river and a herd of wild horses that came up to our campsite in the morning—but I had two days' worth of clothes in a duffel bag and a MasterCard in my wallet. I wanted to see this far part of the state I had ended up in, the wild country where Anna had collected her fossils and cast off a young husband, where something so bad happened that a kind and gentle woman tore off her scabs to make sure she didn't forget.

I drove west on I-94 through Bismarck and then another hundred miles and on past Dickinson, the only other town of any size. The land was treeless and seventeen different shades of tan. It slowly grew more rugged, but the badlands still came up unexpectedly: a crenellation along the horizon that opened up on both sides of the highway into a phantasmagorical landscape. It wasn't so much the buttes rising above the earth, but more as if the skin of the earth had been ripped away, revealing the ragged, broken flesh beneath. You stared *down* into the badlands, and the maze of twisted gorges, trapped meadows, wind-eaten towers and bluffs were a geological underworld, as unearthly as beautiful.

I pulled over at a rest stop to get a better look. Only one other car was parked in the lot. A family of four leaned into the hurricane wind at the railing, the father and son holding their Chicago Cubs caps in place. The boy pointed and I saw something moving deep in the landscape, a line of russet-colored horses disappearing into a keyhole canyon. They were so hard to see against the red and brown country they could have been a hallucination. The mother spotted them through the swirl of her hair and applauded. But as the horses winked out of existence one by one in the shadow of the canyon, I felt the last bit of life leaking out of the day. Now that I was here, the reason for coming had disappeared. What had I thought I'd find? I could drive down to the little town where Anna had grown up, but I had no idea where her farm was or where she had lived once she was married. And what did I think I'd see, anyway? It was a lonely country, but so is any place when things go bad. So is the well-mown lawn inside your own head.

I drove to Medora instead, an old cowboy town that had been remade into a new-and-improved, fake cowboy town. I checked into the Rough Rider Hotel, ate a buffalo steak in the dining room, walked down the street, had an ice-cream cone at a candy-cane-colored shop, and went to bed early.

I couldn't sleep. The air-conditioning slammed on and off and a neon haze drifted in the window from the hotel sign directly below. Somewhere in the middle of the night I felt as if I had come someplace to die, and I thought of my father and the last night he had lain in bed beside my mother, and I wondered if he knew, if he understood what was happening when the stroke hit. I thought about the pain, and wondered how much there was before you could no longer feel it, and these were not good thoughts; these were not things I wanted to think about; this was not my restful vacation. Sometime even deeper in the night I became convinced my father was standing in the corner of the room, watching me with his arms folded, a knowing compassion creasing his dark brow. I could see him clearly in the shadows, but when I sat up in bed, there was nothing there, not even a chair or a coat rack.

The window had shifted from black to blue to indeterminate gray when I got up and dressed. I drove out to Theodore Roosevelt National Park and took the loop road. I had this idea I would climb a butte and watch the sun come up, but light flooded the eastern sky before I had gotten more than a couple of miles into the park. I kept driving. No one else was out. The morning was lovely and still, the air scented with wild sage. I came around a corner to find a buffalo in the middle of the road. A very big buffalo. He stood sideways, filling the pavement, considering me with a baleful eye. I stopped less than two dozen feet from his dusty flank and he didn't move. There was no way around him. We considered each other through the windshield for a while and then I stepped slowly out of the car, which I am sure was a stupid thing to do.

I stood beside the door while he turned his massive head to contemplate me. After due consideration, he seemed to conclude I was unimportant enough that he could go back to staring at whatever he had been staring at on the far side of the road. I took a slow step toward him and then another. Up close his fur was thicker than unshorn wool and matted and dirty and scarred. He was huge and he wasn't any kind of symbol; he wasn't a metaphor; he didn't stand for anything; he didn't feel sent by God or the obscure workings of the universe to deliver any sort of message. He was just a very large animal unimpressed by me, my car, and quite possibly all of history since the saber-toothed tigers had stopped bothering his kind. Here he was, nothing else. He didn't care. He didn't *not* care. He offered no explanation. He just was. I looked at him, breathed in his all-encompassing, ancient smell of earth and dung and hair. He made me smile and then he made me laugh. I backed up carefully, leaned against the car, and waited until he ambled down into the narrow ditch and a cleft between two buttes. I drove the rest of the loop road quickly and headed home to Shannon.

Chapter 21

I HAVE A DAUGHTER NOW. SHE WAS BORN to my wife and me relatively late in life, so she's still young. I usually take a last look in at her when I'm shutting down the house for the night, and, standing there in the glow of her revolving cow night-light, contemplating her sleeping form, the profile that echoes her mother's half hidden behind mussed hair, the skinny arms and legs poking out of a tangle of covers and stuffed animals, I'm overwhelmed by my own sense of vulnerability. I love my wife, and my mother and brother and sister, and, of course, there are other people, old friends, I care about deeply. But when I look in on my daughter, I know I am standing in front of the one part of creation whose loss, I think, would leave me unable to go on.

Helplessness is the essence of unconditional love; you know you would do anything, surrender anything, betray anything. My daughter is a dark star—space and time bend around her until it becomes impossible to see clearly. I believe it is like this for most of us when it comes to our children, but if we are lucky we have chosen someone to have a child with who feels the same way and, in this, there is a shared strength and reassurance that makes it easier. You can turn your attention to the outside world knowing there is someone with you, keeping another eye on the one thing that matters.

If not, if you have to do it on your own, I think you should be forgiven a kind of blindness. The question that always comes up with women who stay with men who hurt them is why. Anna might have had her own answer. I don't know. But I think of her holding the hands of her two children that night they walked toward the Ferris wheel and I think I understand. Here is what I see happening after he first hit her:

Her husband woke up the next morning crosswise on the bed, very nearly dead from alcohol poisoning, and he was silent and sullen and then childishly regretful, sweeping their child too awkwardly into his arms and promising it wouldn't happen again, promising they would make a new start. She saw the boy she had fallen in love with, the mixture of shyness and Southern bravado that had once seemed to promise both safety and escape. And she wanted to believe him so badly she did believe him, and if she believed him a little less the next time, and a little less after that, there was always a hope, one she mocked with increasing bitterness even as she could never quite abandon it. And there was always their child.

Or maybe it was like this:

He woke up the next morning and he was out the door for work without saying a word. He came back that evening, sober and tired and suspicious, as if she had done some injury to him. He was dismissive at dinner and she knew it would never be the same, that a fundamental thing had changed between them. But there was still their child.

Or maybe it was very simple:

She got up early the next morning to leave him. She picked up the baby and she was half a mile down the road before she stopped. She had nowhere to go. And this was their child.

I can imagine any of those mornings, and I can understand the choice in any of them when I look in on my own daughter. But the truth is, I don't know what happened the next day or the day after that. She never told me and there are too many possibilities. All I know is what she said one night as we were working at the light tables.

. . .

THEIR CHILD STARTED TO WALK that fall, and before Anna could imagine how her life might change she was chasing the baby everywhere. There had never been a child that took to running so quickly after walking, never a child so endlessly curious about what might be ahead, just out of sight. That autumn was, for Anna, the autumn of tiny footsteps, a pair of thick little legs disappearing around a corner of the house, high-pitched laughter from somewhere in the green beans, a blond head floating in the brown prairie grass, and sly satisfied giggles from behind the cottonwoods down by the—thank God—dried-up creek.

It was the autumn of sweeping up a small, stocky body against her chest and feeling the surprisingly strong kick of legs that wanted to keep going, wanted to keep moving. She was very happy, Anna said, to be watching their child grow up in the country she loved, and she was also terrified by how it was a land without fences, how it went on and on, and there was nothing, really, to stop anyone—any creature that was mobile—

from disappearing into it forever. She learned to hang out the laundry, do her gardening, walk down the road to the mailbox, with one part of her always tracing the small steps by her side, one part of her focused on the hand in hers. The nightmare that woke her at night, gasping for breath, was of feeling, a second too late, that her hand was empty, of looking down and realizing she held nothing but air.

Every parent has to learn you can't hold on all the time, and she didn't, but she developed an invisible tether that tugged at her if her firstborn strayed too far. Yet at the same time she was proud, very proud, of the pint-sized exploring spirit that paraded away from her without looking back, that charged into the world at every chance as if there were a danger the planet might escape before it could be properly explored. "Always running," she said. "Always curious. Always wanting to see . . . "

Telling me about these months, she made it sound as if it were just the two of them, living on her garden and wild raspberries in the trailer in the valley in the badlands. And maybe that was what made it all possible, creating a separate peace, severing the days from whatever happened at night when her husband came home.

. . .

EMILY'S CAR WAS PARKED on the street when I returned from my restful vacation. She was sitting in the living room reading a paperback with a flat green cover. When I came into the room she dropped it wearily onto the floor.

"God, I hate this shit."

"What is it?"

"A book."

I went into the bathroom and when I came back she had turned her gaze to the window. I got a glass of water and pulled the stool from the kitchen counter over to sit next to her.

"You can't just keep showing up. You have to call. And it's not always going to work out to visit."

I had surprised and hurt her, at least a little, but she didn't want to admit it.

"I thought it was just kind of easy for both of us," she said.

"Yeah. That doesn't really make it good."

"But not bad."

"No."

I followed her gaze out the window. The unlit neon sign of the Buffalo Bar, the tarred rooftops broken by rusted metal vents, the cyanic North Dakota sky.

"What are you doing?" I asked. "What are you doing all day here? What do you do when you disappear from here?"

Her full mouth pursed slightly. "I kinda started taking a couple of classes again." She nodded toward the book on the floor.

"Do you like it? I mean, is it what you want to be doing?"

Her hair had grown out into an unkempt blonde tangle that reached her shoulders and was always falling into her eyes. She brushed it out of the way.

"I don't know—I like it as much as I ever did. I like it better than all the other things I could be doing. It was never for me like it is for you, Ricky. I never knew what I wanted to do. I never had a thing I loved doing. College was just a way to avoid other stuff."

"Hold it," I said. "I didn't have some thing I *loved*. I didn't know what I wanted to do. I still don't."

For the first time since I had come into the room Emily looked at me fondly. "You were always so smart and such an idiot. Sure you do." She waved her hand to take in the town. "All this."

"My goal was to sit and stare out a window at some nowhere little town?"

"What you do here. What you're *doing*. You're so lucky, Ricky. You have this. I thought we might start over. But I guess you can't, really."

"I'm not sure we really even started," I said.

"Mean."

"No, I don't mean it like that. I just see people"—and I thought of all the couples I had come to know in this small town, Paul and his wife, Todd and Christina, even Art and Louise—"and I just think they have something that, you know . . . we don't."

Emily was quiet for a long time.

"Okay."

She stood up and went into the bedroom. It took her only a minute to gather her things while I stood in the doorway. She packed the way she did everything, with a kind of goofy, haphazard grace that tugged at my heart even as the halfhearted nature of it all remained a mystery. I thought about how you could watch someone brush her teeth, watch her undress, feel her crawl into bed beside you, listen to her breathing, feel her cheek pressed against your shoulder, her arms wrapped around you for comfort, and not know her at all. I know this is commonplace wisdom, but there is a first time you have to learn it, and it hurts.

"You never told me what happened with . . ." I honestly couldn't remember his name again.

"Ted."

"Yeah."

Emily threw a T-shirt into her duffel bag, rummaged through the bedcovers, and found a stray sock. "I thought he might be the thing. He thought Giselle, the new waitress, might be the thing, at least for a couple of nights, until some other new thing came along. But Giselle, she once thought somebody else might be the thing, and that somebody had a disease, and then Ted did and I did, and you don't, you know, because I took care of it, and that wasn't so nice because I got infected, and I actually had to spend a couple of days in the hospital, which would be just fairly sucky, anyway, but he never came by once, and that was when I knew I wasn't the thing and he wasn't the thing, and I really had no thing. Nothing at all."

She zipped up the bag a little too hard.

"Like I said, you're lucky."

"It's just a job, Emily. That's all it is."

She shook her head impatiently. "Think about it, Ricky."

I followed her to the front door. She hesitated and gave me a quick, bony hug.

"I'm not going to call, you know."

"I know."

"All right. Hey—"

"Hey—"

I did stand in the window and watch her get in her car and

drive down the street, and I can't say it was without sadness or a sense of loss. Life seemed filled with people disappearing, and she was right: it hadn't been bad. It just hadn't been enough. I moved the stool back beside the counter and grabbed a sponge and wiped down the counter, and then I straightened the furniture and the books and found a rag under the sink and dusted everything, which I can't be certain but I believe may have been the first time I ever dusted in my life. I stood, at the end, in the middle of the small and barely furnished room, flooded with an unfamiliar and comforting sense of possession. My place.

Chapter 22

Anna's kids sometimes came tumbling into the office at the end of the school day, Stephen always serious and respectful, as if he was conscious of disturbing a place of work, Sam loud and happy. She loved to sit down at an empty typewriter and clatter away until I had to fight off the urge to grab her by the seat of her pants and throw her back out the door.

She had a routine with Louise whenever they bumped into each other.

"Sign that kid up," Louise would say, fixing Sam with her solar eye. "She's a natural!"

Sam would stare happily back into the eye as if it were a portal into a funhouse dimension and pound even harder on the keys. When she was particularly inspired she would utter phrases she had either picked up on the evening news or heard her mother mutter under her breath. My favorite was, "Deadlines deadlines *deadlines*."

Louise would nod gravely and disappear into the back,

always returning a second later with cans of Orange Crush for both kids.

"Drink up!" she would order Sam. "You need the energy if you're going to work at this paper, young woman. We have fun, but we work hard around here!"

"Say thank you," Anna would gently prod her daughter with a look of quiet affection, and this is something I want you to understand: The scenes that happen off-camera in Anna's story are overwhelmingly scenes of love. She was a mother, first of all, and her children were the largely unseen center of each day. I think about that now, and I think about how hard it must have been. A single mother. Not much money, never enough, really. A life like millions of others in America, equally off-camera. Imagine her tending to a thousand small things in her small house on the sere edge of town—tennis shoes, textbooks, homework, stomach flus, birthday parties, bills—and you have the part of her story we don't see. This was Anna's heart, and that makes the mystery of her end even harder to understand because she loved them fiercely, protected them with every ounce of her will every day. I am sure of this.

Yet in the end it wasn't enough and, with apologies to Robert Frost, the question is not fire or ice; they are both a kind of beckoning flame; the question is how the gentle, sustaining light leaks out of life.

. . .

IN MY MEMORY the days now fly toward winter. Football season starts and I spend part of each Friday driving past combines crisscrossing ripened fields, heading toward a rectangle of dying grass at the edge of another small town where teenage boys in faded jerseys and battered helmets pummel themselves black and blue under lights that lend the scene the stark, judgmental quality of crime scene photos. Anna didn't care for the game, didn't understand its rules, hated its violence, so I returned to my first job as a sports reporter, standing on the sidelines, shivering as the sun went down. I still had all my other work, of course, but I found I didn't mind surrendering my Friday nights to the games. The smallest towns didn't even have stands; the crowds bunched around the fields, cheering fiercely to stay warm, the sound tribal, ancient, and somehow reassuring.

This parade of days slows down twice. The first time came early in the fall when Todd and I were shooting baskets on a Sunday morning in the park. A handful of high school kids joined us and after I made a nice fade-away shot, I heard one of them say to a buddy, "Not bad for an old guy."

I had turned twenty-one a few days earlier, a birthday I couldn't celebrate properly since I had been drinking illegally in the Buffalo Bar for months. Hearing the kid, I felt that I had stepped across a line drawn on the court and committed myself to the team on the other side. The feeling only grew stronger after the kids left and Todd and I were idly tossing the ball toward the hoop.

"I think I'm engaged," he said.

I had been about to shoot, but I let the ball fall.

"What? Really?"

"Yeah." Todd shrugged, as if admitting he had done something sort of silly, like painting a room purple.

"Okay. I mean . . . *What?*"

"Christine and I were talking last night and, well, I guess, she asked and I sort of . . . you know . . ."

I knew they had been seeing a lot of each other. I knew she was at his place a lot, and I knew it seemed to be working for both of them, but I hadn't thought of it working quite *that* well.

"Wait a minute. So she asked you to marry her and you said yes?"

Todd picked up the ball and tossed it to me.

"She didn't *propose*. I'm not that lame, man, that some girl has to ask me to marry her. Christine asked me what I thought about us, how I thought it was going, and we were just lying there talking and it sort of, you know, got to that point."

I tossed the ball back at him.

"So *you* proposed?"

"Well, I didn't get down on my knees or anything. I mean, we were already lying there and, you know, naked, so it would have been kind of awkward."

We sat down on the bench beside the court.

"I just kind of said, you know, I thought it was good, really good, and she said she thought so, too, and she asked me if I ever thought about having a family someday, and you know, I like kids, and, well . . . I'm kind of engaged, I think."

We contemplated the red and gold trees on the periphery of the park.

"This isn't like the vacuum cleaners, is it?"

He squinted at me. "What do you mean?"

"Something you think you want to do until you do it."

"No. It's not like that at all." He kicked the ball. "It's not like that. But it is a big thing. It's kind of scary."

"No shit."

"Yeah, but, you know. You can't just live like a single guy forever. It gets old."

I nodded.

"So, if I am engaged, you wanna be my best man?"

"Yeah, no, sure. I mean—it's an honor."

"Cool."

I stood and chased the ball down, tossed it toward the basket. Todd followed me.

"You should have gotten down on your knees."

Todd caught the rebound and banked it back in, the ball falling through the net with that beautiful sound.

"Man, the floor in that room is *freezing.*"

I saw Christina that noon in the café.

"Congratulations . . . I think."

She held her coffeepot up, ready to dump the contents in my lap.

"You better be happy for us, Ricky."

I held up my hands. "I am. I'm just a little unclear on the details."

"We're getting married in November. It's going to be a small wedding. At Grace Lutheran. You and Todd will be wearing dark suits, not tuxedos. We'll have a reception in the back here. Appetizers and drinks. I've talked to Rosie and she's going to give us the room for free, but we'll have to pay for the booze. It's going to run from eight to midnight and then we'll leave on our honeymoon. I hope we can go to San Diego. I'd like to see the ocean. I've never seen the ocean."

"Okay," I said. "That does clear things up."

She lowered the coffee a couple of inches.

"You have a suit?"

"I have a suit. I'll have to go home and get it, but I have a suit."

"Good. Great." She set the coffeepot on the edge of the table and I could see she was on the edge of crying. "It's going to be *wonderful.*"

. . .

THE OTHER THING that slows the rush of days is the change in Anna. It happened over time, but I think it started early, the first day I was back in the office after my brief vacation out West. Louise wanted to know how it had gone—my healing trip to a lake in Minnesota. I told her the fishing had been *fantastic* and proceeded to go into detail. I was somewhere in the middle of a story about fighting a ten-pound walleye for twenty minutes on a reel with five-pound line when I saw Anna shaking her head at me. The fish promptly spit the hook and escaped into the Minnesota wilderness, the way all the best fish stories end.

"Where did you really go?" Anna asked when we were pasting up the paper.

"Your neck of the woods," I said, "or rather, neck without woods. Medora. Teddy Roosevelt National Park. I saw a buffalo."

She looked as if she was trying to decide whether to believe me.

"You went west? . . . A buffalo?"

"Big one. Smelled like an old rug."

"*Smelled?* How close did you get?"

"A couple of feet." An acceptable exaggeration, I thought, after willfully surrendering a ten-pound walleye to her caution.

"You stayed in the car, right?"

"Nope."

Anna shook her head again. "Sometimes you're like twelve years old. You could have been gored or trampled, you know."

I thought briefly about trying to explain how it had been. How it had been a living breathing creature that was like a mountain or a sky filled with majestic clouds, a thing that told you the world was what it was and you and your sorrows didn't matter that much, really, in the face of what was maybe simply a great uncaring, but also a great beauty. But of course I didn't really think all that, at least not clearly—I only think it now, many years later. At the time, I only knew I felt somehow better, maybe even a little smug.

"Yep. It was great."

"It was?"

"Yep."

"Did I say twelve? Maybe ten," she said. "How did Emily react to you taking your life in your hands?"

"I don't know," I said. "She left."

Anna had been about to set a strip of copy onto a page. Her hand stopped in midair.

"She left?"

"I asked her to leave. Move out."

I was trying to keep my voice light—trying to hold on to my newborn sense of release from the dull weight of the last months—and maybe I came across as too flip because I had thought she would be pleased: I was taking steps, I was moving on, I was not settling. But her tone was brittle.

"Just like that. You sent her on her way."

"I guess, I mean . . . yes, just like that. Sort of."

"And that was easy."

"Well," I said too brightly, "it had to be done, right?"

Anna resumed laying the copy on the page, the same careful movement I had always seen, and yet there was a vagueness, a sense of confusion as her hands came off the table, returned, straightened the story, lifted it, tried again. She picked up another strip of copy, set it down, and walked without explanation into the front shop, where she was gone much longer than necessary.

That was the start. Her mood darkened as the days shortened, which makes it sound like it makes sense, but the autumn in North Dakota is the best of seasons: The afternoons swell with diffused light, the trees are kaleidoscopes, the sky cracks gently along the edge, and all the colors spill into early evening. It's a time when the unexpected perfection of a particular day can stop you in midstride, when your thoughts slow down to take on a renewed clarity and you make a series of small resolutions to do better from here on out as you turn up your collar against the approaching winter.

I recall that autumn as particularly bright and mild. For Anna, though, a reef of clouds seemed to be building on the horizon. It wasn't an all-at-once change, but a shading away from the woman I had known. I was still facing my own dark moments—it wasn't like the placid disregard of one buffalo in the Wild West had swept them clean—so I was slow to accept the difference. I felt it but avoided thinking about it. Anna stood only a few feet away on Thursdays, still ordering the news of our little world into neat columns, and if she was quieter, sharper, or impatient, more often absent, I tried to pretend it wasn't happening. I tried to chat the way we had, told the kind of jokes that once made her smile. Everyone needs to believe in at least one adult, and she was mine. I made myself believe nothing had really changed.

So it was a surprise when Christina called me after ten one evening, her voice unsteady, and asked if we could meet at the Buffalo Bar. I crossed the street thinking something had happened between her and Todd and that I was absolutely the wrong person to be turning to for condolences or romantic advice, since I was lousy at the first and had nothing but failure to draw on for the second.

Christine was sitting alone at a table by the door.

"Anna won't be my maid of honor."

I looked at her blankly.

"It's like the best man for the bride, you *idiot*."

"Oh . . . What? . . . Really?"

"She said she doesn't do weddings."

This was all coming a little too fast. I wished I had gotten a beer from the bar before sitting down.

"She doesn't *do* weddings. What does that mean? It's not *her* wedding. It's mine."

"I don't—"

"I thought she was my friend. I thought we were *best* friends."

Howard, the bartender, was staring uncertainly at our table, and I realized Christina was crying. This had somehow escaped my trained journalistic powers of observation.

"Listen. Hold it! Hang on. She *is* your friend. I know that. I don't . . . I don't know why she won't do it, but I don't think it has anything to do with you. I don't think it has anything to do with being your friend or . . . whatever. I think it has to do with her. Her own life. There are things she's scared of. I mean, things she just can't . . ." As I was saying all this, I was seeing it myself, seeing the men Anna had turned away, seeing the body language that held her carefully apart, remembering the way she stood in the back, near a door, at birthday parties or any celebration, really.

Christina brushed her tears away so roughly I thought she was going to leave scars. She slid her beer across the table toward me and I realized I had somehow managed to say the right thing.

"I know that, you idiot. I know all about that *asshole* and everything he did to her. But I thought . . . for my wedding. I mean, Todd, too. For *our* wedding—"

"Would you like me to talk to her?"

I had never really noticed, but Christina, tough-girl haircut and all, looked about twelve when she smiled.

Chapter 23

BUT I DIDN'T TALK TO ANNA. The next day the high school principal resigned and there were rumors of missing money and an office romance, a secretary who had gained a suspicious amount of weight before disappearing on an extended leave. Small towns come with a hardwired rumor circuit that trips in and operates at light speed in such circumstances, and Edith, who drew on people she had known for a hundred years, and I both spent day and night trying to sort through the ever more bizarre stories buzzing through Shannon.

I had one good source on the school board and I was finally able to determine that the secretary's leave of absence was, indeed, a pregnancy, but had nothing to do with the principal. Stolen money wasn't an issue, although there had been an ongoing disagreement between the chairman of the board and the principal about the budget. The real reason the avuncular, balding man in badly checked sport coats, whom I'd considered the embodiment of a small-town school administrator, was leaving was that his wife had stomach cancer, and they were moving to

Arizona so she could pursue alternative treatment. She didn't want anyone to know she was sick because she didn't want to be a bother.

The night they agreed to talk to me about this, they asked that I park down the street and come up the alley to their house. "Everybody knows your car," the principal said, and I felt strangely notorious. The school board member who had first tipped me to the truth was waiting inside with them. The principal's wife insisted on serving coffee and putting out lemon cookies while I listened to her husband and realized from the defeat in his eyes that he didn't believe in her decision and thought she was going to die.

His wife sat down on the overstuffed couch beside him. "It's all become too much of a commotion," she said, picking at a thread on the cuff of her loose-knit sweater. "You'll have to tell people, I guess, but could you just tell them I'm sick and we're going down for treatment? I don't want to have to go over all the details with every nosy nobody."

I walked back down the alley and sat in my car on a street of neatly kept pillbox houses all nearly identical to theirs. A small-town street at night. Yellow porch lights above concrete steps. Shadows of life moving behind curtained windows. Silence like an old, comfortable sweater. I wondered how many of her friends had noticed how thin she had become and not said a thing, or asked so obliquely that the question had been as easy to set aside as a teacup. I sat in my car thinking about a woman who viewed dying as an embarrassment, and the fragile peace I had made with my own grief unraveled. My heart simmered and then raged at the inbred reticence of the people in this state, the reflexive politeness that said nothing, the vapid declarations about weather and last night's game used to build small, neat pillboxes of emotional shelter. I wanted someone to tell me they had no idea what they were doing. I wanted someone to say they were scared to death. I wanted someone to say they were going out of their mind trying to cope. I wanted someone to get too loud, to start shouting and not be able to stop.

I thought I might start by admitting I'd been a coward. I'd had a week to talk to Anna and I hadn't because I had no idea what to say and I didn't want to know the reason why she couldn't face Christina's wedding. I was no better than the rest. I didn't want to know and I was mad she hadn't told me. Wasn't I her friend? Her good friend? I turned the key, slipped the gearshift into neutral, and raced the engine, letting the whole world know I was here, and drove up the hill to Anna's house.

The lights were still on. She opened the door in her robe, and for a moment her smallness, the vulnerability and the sensuality of her half-undressed self, stopped me, but I was heedless. I asked if I could come in. Anna looked disconcerted and told me to wait a moment. When she opened the door again she had pulled on jeans and a denim work shirt.

"I found out the truth about Hartness," I said. "His wife's got cancer. They're leaving town so she can get treatment."

Anna was still unsettled, running a hand through her bedroom hair. Her voice was even softer than usual.

"Is it bad?"

"She's going to die. They're going to Arizona so she can try some alternative medicine bullshit."

"God."

"She asked me not to tell people the details. I have no idea what I'm going to write."

Anna walked to a small chest of drawers in the corner. She fished around and pulled out a pack of cigarettes, held one in her hand, set it down, picked it up, and brought it back to the couch unlit, avoiding my eyes.

"Why wouldn't you help with the story?"

"Eric. What?"

"Why wouldn't you help? Every time I asked, you made some excuse and disappeared. We could have used the help."

Anna stared at the cigarette, halfway to her mouth. "I don't smoke in the house."

"And why won't you be Christina's best maid?"

She set the cigarette down with a small, pained smile. "Maid of honor."

"Whatever. Why not? And don't tell me you don't do weddings. She's your friend."

Anna looked at me then, an odd desperation in her eyes.

"You come to my house, get me out of bed, to ask me this? Eric . . . please . . ."

"I told Christina I'd talk to you. Just tell me why."

She closed her eyes. Water trickled in a pipe somewhere in the back of the house.

"I'll do it."

"I don't care. Just tell me why."

"I'll do it, Eric."

"I don't care. I just want to know *why*. Tell me why you said no the first time. Tell me why this is such a hard thing to do."

"I've told you," Anna said. "I've even shown you."

And I knew she had and I had known she had and I didn't understand why I was sitting in her living room near midnight so angry I could hardly speak. And I didn't understand how that anger could so suddenly dissipate, leaving only this faint taste of ash in the back of my throat.

"It's just standing in the front of a church," I said, "for a friend."

Anna stared into a corner as if waiting for something or someone to appear. The house was quiet all around us.

"You better go. We'll wake up the kids."

"Listen—"

"It's late, Eric."

She led me to the door.

"The reason I didn't help with the story," she said, "is because I didn't want to know if the things they were saying were true. I think people should be allowed to keep some things to themselves."

And she shut the door quietly, but firmly, in my face.

Chapter 24

THAT WAS THE BEGINNING of the winter in Anna. Autumn stretched into November with no snow, the days cold and clear, but she had been stolen from the season, the woman who didn't do well in snow buried in some private whiteout I only half understood. We worked together as before, but on Thursday nights we only talked about work or small, inessential things. Afterward I lay in bed alone and in my head I played over what I said or could have said to her, as if different words might have made a difference, as if there were magic words that could change whatever had happened between us.

During the day she appeared to be struggling, for the first time, to finish her articles, disappearing longer than she should have on assignments, reworking short pieces laboriously. She developed a sinus infection that lingered for days, and the weather seemed to worsen her arthritis. She looked no different and yet there was this sense each hour was taking ten out of her. Out of the corner of my eye I would watch her set down her coffee cup, pick up a pencil, hold it above a page, set it down again, close her eyes with the effort, and it all seemed hard, as if every object had been transformed into lead.

Late one afternoon I couldn't find the print of a photo she had taken that I planned for the front page. I knew Anna would know where it was, but she wasn't in the back shop or the darkroom. Edith thought maybe she'd walked to the drugstore.

"I need that photo," I said, grabbing my jacket off the coatrack, as Edith, working at the desk next to Anna's deserted one, raised a skeptical eyebrow.

A fall chill hung in the air as I walked downtown. The street was quiet, damp leaves scattered like smears of paint on the sidewalk. The missing photograph was beautiful, a wooden railroad bridge to the east of town at the end of day, the pilings and leafless trees silhouetted against a flattened sun hovering just above the river's bank. I didn't really need the print until Thursday, as Edith knew, but a growing impatience had overtaken me. I thought maybe I would meet Anna coming back from Main Street and we could walk back to the paper together. It would be good to be out of the office, outside, and maybe we would talk. I had a vision of the two of us walking back slowly, appreciating Shannon in the hushed silence while the day turned a dreamlike blue-gray around us. Whatever it was that had happened to Anna, happened between us, dissolving in the same gentle light.

Instead I met Louise marching down the middle of the sidewalk before I reached the business district.

"Heading home, Ricky?"

"I was looking for Anna," I said, realizing it sounded slightly odd as I said it.

But Louise nodded. "Well." She pivoted slowly, hands on hips, looking back down the sidewalk as if an army of Annas might be sneaking up on us. "I believe she has gone home. She wasn't feeling well."

"Oh, okay."

We stood there. She filled up the sidewalk so there was no graceful way to step around her, yet I didn't really want to walk back to the office together. She'd never mentioned the day I found her in the back of her paper forest, never said another word about Art's friends. I wasn't even sure she remembered talking to me, but I dreaded the possibility of further confidences, and I'd been avoiding being alone with her ever since. Now here we were, together on the quietest afternoon in the last hundred years.

"Seasonal affective disorder," Louise said firmly.

"What?"

"It's a well-known medical condition, Ricky. It's hard to get enough sunlight when the days get shorter. It affects your mood."

I knew what it was, and I knew it wasn't Anna's problem. But I couldn't think of what to say. We stared at each other awkwardly, seeing each other a little too well.

"It's not so easy to live in this climate," Louise said, taking a deep noisy breath and looking around. "Or in this small town. People have to learn to deal with it. I think you're going to have to exercise a little patience. A good editor knows when to give his people some space."

I had never thought of Anna as "my people," but if I had people, she was it.

"I just had a question to ask her. It's no big deal."

Louise nodded. "Well. Good." She pounded her fists together as if waiting for me to join her on her energetic march back to the office.

"Yeah, I think I'll just grab something uptown before coming back."

When Louise was half a block away I stopped and watched her. The light was falling fast and she cast an oversized shadow that stretched across the dead grass—an impressive figure, even in retreat. We were never going to talk about that night, but she remembered.

. . .

THE WEDDING CAME UP in this twilight like an iceberg in the North Atlantic. Suddenly I was rushing home to get my one and only dark suit, finding it fit loosely, and realizing I had lost weight in the last year. My mother stood in the doorway while I slipped the jacket on and in her quietly startled sadness I knew she was seeing the ghost of her young husband, perhaps even on his wedding day, and I wished that could be true for her, that for one last day I could be replaced by the man she had known. I'd have happily stepped out of existence for that.

Instead, I was just some schmo of a best man who had to come up with a toast and not lose the ring and attend to a dozen small acts of patience and false cheer with a bride who grew only slightly more hysterical and a groom who grew quite a bit more baffled as the Big Day slid up to our little ship and then slammed hard into the side.

On his wedding day Todd somehow managed to lose the

black dress shoes he had bought especially for the occasion. He called in a panic while I was drinking my morning coffee. It was Sunday, of course. The only clothing store in Shannon was closed, and the nearest city was too far away, and after searching every corner of every closet in his house I found the shoes in a kitchen drawer sitting in the middle of his frying pan and handed them to him without asking.

"They need to be polished," he said, sounding as if he had just realized he had to disassemble a jet engine.

"Jesus Christ, I'll do it."

"Thanks, man. Thanks."

"Where's the polish?"

"Oh, shit, I have no *idea*!"

"It's okay. I have some . . . I think. I'll get it." I took the shoes carefully out of his hands. "Listen. It's ten a.m. You've got to calm down a bit."

Christina had made him get a haircut, but it hadn't turned out that well. His wiry hair stuck out here and there like a badly mowed pasture. He scratched nervously at the back of his head and then ran both hands through his hair until it had come to full alert.

"I hate being all in front of people and everything."

"Everybody does"—I shook my head—". . . except maybe politicians."

He stared at me blankly.

"Politicians," I said, "they like being up in front of people."

"I'm not a politician! I don't want to be a *politician*! Oh, shit, Ricky, what am I doing getting *married?*"

"Wait. Hold it. It's not just politicians who get married."

"Right."

"*People* get married."

"Right. *Right*."

It dawned on me that he had been looking for his shoes in his dress shirt and slacks, with his tie badly knotted at his neck.

"What are you doing getting dressed at ten a.m., anyway?"

"I don't want to be late."

"The wedding's at two."

"Right. *Right*. Lots of time."

"Yeah."

We stared at each other. I was still holding the shoes.

"I'm going to go get some polish. You should take off the tie. You'll just get it dirty."

When I got back Todd was sprawled on the couch in his boxer shorts, drinking a Budweiser and watching the Minnesota Vikings on television.

"Thanks, man." He took a long swig. "Bit of a panic attack. It's cool. You're right. We're just people."

. . .

WE WERE STANDING in a tiny room in the front of the church, waiting to go on with the preacher, who looked about my age. The silence had started to wear thin, so I asked him how he could counsel people on marriage when he was single himself, which was maybe not the wisest right-before-wedding query.

"I don't need to jump off a cliff to tell people not to commit suicide," he said, looking vaguely self-satisfied.

Todd turned two shades whiter, which I would not have believed possible.

"She's a wonderful young woman," the preacher said. "You've made a great choice."

I suddenly couldn't breathe all that well. I stepped to the door, open just a crack, and watched the church fill up. Edith marched down the aisle, ignoring the usher, studying the pastel-blue program instead. I could imagine her already composing the social note she would type up for the paper. Paul was next, his wife and two kids following along. I'd never seen him in a suit before and he looked as sober and responsible as a banker, no sign of ink beneath his fingernails. Someday, I realized, Art would sell him the print shop and everybody there would be working for him. A vaguely strangled sound came from behind me and I glanced back to see Todd and the preacher staring at each other like a pair of cats that had stumbled into each other in an alley. When I looked back into the church Art and Louise were being led to a pew, Louise in a hat that seemed to have a peacock feather with a bright purple eye rising a foot into the air and swooping back over her square shoulders. It made her look like the grandmother of one of the Three Musketeers. Art was wearing a seersucker suit, although the day was chilly, and bright red suspenders that had been attached a little too close to his belly button, lending him the air of a slightly disheveled Austrian flügelhorn player. They were holding hands, and as they settled into a pew near the front, an unexpected wave of affection surged over me. There they all were: Edith, Paul, everyone from the café, the bar, the entire court of the strange little kingdom to which I had pledged my fealty, led by our puttering count and his fierce countess, who now had one blue, one red, and one purple eye.

I felt Todd's presence at my shoulder.

"Oh, God. People."

"You're people, remember?"

Out of the corner of my eye I saw him nod without conviction. He was too scared, and I was his best man.

"You want to make a break for it?" I said.

A slightly-too-long silence.

"What?"

"Run for it. Flee. Canada's only a couple of hours away."

"I don't know Canadian."

"You can pick it up. I'll hold them off."

I heard him release a long, unsteady breath.

"Naah."

"Sure?"

"Yeah."

The organist hit the first notes in the back of the church.

"Good," I said. "Because we're on."

Standing up front beside the altar, I felt strangely light and very nearly invisible. It struck me that the best man could wear a purple wig and a clown's nose and it was unlikely anyone would notice; the groom himself could probably get away with the nose. Instead we stood in our dark suits like a pair of cheerful apprentice undertakers. I looked through the arched window across from me at a pine tree, solitary and still in its frame of gray sky and dead grass, and realized it had started to snow. The organist turned to the magisterial opening of the processional. We squared our shoulders and faced the aisle.

The flower girl came first, a previously unknown niece of Christina's. Then Anna. You see people anew in circumstances like that and I was struck by the odd contrasts in her beauty, the delicacy of her features and frame, the coarse thickness of her hair, and the earthy tint of her skin, the solidity in the way she carried herself, a farm girl, still, and yet how small she really was. She floated inside the frills of her chiffon, pastel-peach dress, which was no worse than any bridesmaid's dress I have seen since, but seemed particularly mismatched with this woman I had never seen wear anything but dark colors. She held her eyes in front of her, not even glancing at her children, who I saw now were sitting in the same pew as Edith, but keeping her gaze fixed a few feet over our heads. She wore a small, set smile, and I wondered if anyone else saw the pain in her eyes.

Anna reached the other side of the altar and turned to wait for the bride. She managed a brief, meant-to-be-reassuring smile for Todd, but looked past me as if I were invisible. The wedding march started and we all came to attention.

. . .

ANNA FLED HER MARRIAGE sometime in the winter. I don't know the details. I only know she ran away to Bismarck, which is the state capital and the closest thing to a city for three hundred miles in any direction if you live in western North Dakota. She took their child and she moved into the spare bedroom in the apartment of a high school classmate, who had taken a job in an insurance office.

She left and she came back and her parents tried to convince her to stay and she ended up pounding her own blood into a sink full of raw meat and she left again, but her parents drove to

Bismarck to talk to her, and so did he, and she came back again. The same trailer. The same valley in the middle of nowhere. She stood in the kitchen in the late afternoon dark, amazed at how little time had really passed. Still winter. The welt on her husband's shoulder from a chain that had snapped loose on a rig still a bright red.

He came straight home at the end of the working day and sat at the small kitchen table like a child who has been told to be still. He watched her making dinner with a carefully attentive gaze, as if there might be a test later. When their child tugged at the door to the outdoors, ready to take off on an adventure in the winter countryside, he swept the baby up in his arms, hiding a plastic cow in one hand or the other as a distraction. He finally shooed the child away with an overly gentle pat on the bottom and resumed following her cooking. His attention made her nervous. She could feel his restlessness like a hunger, and she could feel how hard he was trying to be present, how hard he was trying to be good. She sensed this was part of some last, frightened attempt to locate a better self, and it scared her so badly she tipped over the macaroni box, spilling pieces across the stove and into the burner, where they flared and curled up to die.

She heard the chair tip over from being pushed back too quickly and braced herself for the blow, but his knotted bicep appeared on the counter beside her as he swept the remaining pieces into his other hand. Trying to help. She dared to look over her shoulder and his face was close, and so sad, desperate and lost, she found she dared to speak.

"It's okay. I can do it."

He stepped back and stood there helplessly. She swept the last of the macaroni away, turned down the burner, and faced him.

"Thank you."

He poured himself a small shot of Jack Daniel's before dinner and sipped it carefully while they ate across the small table from each other, the child in the high chair between them, to her right and his left. He came to the end of his bourbon as they finished eating and stood to refill his glass. When he sat back down he had filled two with another modest shot each. He slid one toward her.

"Have a drink with me. Please."

There was such desperation, such a subdued, childlike longing, in his request she lifted the glass and took a sip, closing her eyes briefly as the small fuse it lit burned its way into her chest. When she opened her eyes he was smiling. She took another drink, feeling the flame trace itself past her heart. He took a small swallow and in his fragile happiness she saw the boy she had first fallen for in the green light of the dashboard, and she thought that maybe this was marriage. Maybe this was the kind of thing you had.

• • •

WE MARCHED OUT OF THE CHURCH and there was snow swirling down from the heavens and rice on a considerably lower trajectory and, for some reason, popcorn tossed by the contingent from the Buffalo Bar. Todd held Christina's hand and I thought he might swing her down the steps and possibly right over the car, so happy and relieved did he look. They skipped down the steps together instead and rice stuck in their hair and popcorn bounced off their shoulders and when his eyes caught mine in a brief, absolutely confident glance, I shook my head and started to laugh because this was love, and it was possible, and it happened, and you had to believe in it, after all. You had to believe that people could actually find each other and take the chance and do the right thing. Step out into thin air together.

I'd walked out arm in arm with Anna, and I turned to her now to share the moment, but she was gone.

Chapter 25

THE NEXT NIGHT HER HUSBAND CAME home only a little late, bringing with him a bottle of wine with a straw basket wrapped around its bulbous shape. He was excited by the purchase, proud of it, and they drank the bottle during dinner, taking turns leaving the table to steer the child back into the room. The wind was blowing hard enough to twist the trailer on its metal skeleton. As they drank, Anna felt it was as if they were on a wooden sailing boat making its way across an endless sea, and she saw the spark of romance in her husband's eyes, and later that night in bed she felt the ice-cold wind that slipped past the rattling window frame along her back as she rose over him and, as she shivered in the mingling of heat and cold, felt she was reclaiming some lost part of her existence, something she needed to believe was worth the price she could distantly feel tallying in her future.

I don't know this, of course. I can't really know any of this. I can only imagine how it must have been. All I know is she told me they started drinking together and for a while it was good again. "The house fell apart," she said in the distant way she sometimes had when talking about her own past, as if she had peered into a microscope to discover a strange, alien life. "The dishes were always sitting in the sink and nothing got cleaned. But I thought it was better. We were together. I knew we couldn't keep living like this, but I thought it might be working. I thought we could make it work."

. . .

TODD AND CHRISTINA WENT away on their honeymoon and when they returned they were badly sunburned and happier than ever. Paul and I spent a day helping them move everything out of Christina's apartment into Todd's house, and at the end she kissed me on the cheek and hugged me so fiercely I felt embarrassed and offered to stay and help rearrange the furniture.

I saw them less as they cocooned themselves into their life together, but when I was over there, for dinner, or stopping by after work, I saw the honeymoon pictures on the bookcase and in the evening the wedding china set out on the table and over the weeks the pounds slowly filling out Todd's frame, and this, too, was a lesson, a glance into the quiet, physical accretion of happiness in contented lives, and I saw for the first time how this could be, how this *was* for someone not much older than I was. When Christina lit the candles around their new dining room table and poured cheap wine into brand-new long-stemmed glasses and Todd raised one in a brief, half-embarrassed toast, I knew I wanted to be doing this someday around my own table.

My own apartment was empty when I came home at night. The Buffalo Bar felt empty, too. Without Todd and Christina, it was just me and the old men playing pool, and pretty soon I only went when I couldn't face eating dinner alone. I sat at the bar one evening in late December, watching the *Monday Night Football* game, eating chili, and sipping a beer. Bart Tollesrud, who had worked at the bomb factory on the edge of town since it opened, was sitting on the next stool, eating the same chili, drinking the same beer. He had a coarse, three-day growth of beard and watery eyes glued to the game. A spot of chili dripped into his beard; he wiped it away absently with his flannel sleeve, and I saw the ghost of a possible future self and had to leave without taking the time to pay. They would just put it on my tab anyway.

. . .

ANNA WAS NEARLY SILENT on our Thursday evenings together. She often appeared a little late, and when she was there, she seemed preoccupied, as if this world were a thin, translucent gauze laid over a real and more disturbing landscape invisible to the rest of us. When I stubbornly tried to reignite our old rambling conversations she sometimes looked up at me as if I had startled her by my presence, and then as if the mere fact of my being in the room caused her pain.

Something had changed in me, too. I no longer had so many opinions about the world and its easily marked idiocies. A strange feeling of suspension had crept into my judgment. I was no longer so sure; I wanted more time to think about it—all of it.

I was finishing the layout on a page, and a ghost in a photograph caught my eye. It was a picture of the county commission posing outside a newly completed vehicle barn for county equipment, the most dreadfully boring picture you could imagine, really. But the barn was on the edge of town and in the far distance, in the back of the photograph, a man could be seen sitting in the snow on the side of a hill. At least I thought it was a man. He sat in a gray parka, the hood pulled up around his hidden face, and from his posture he seemed to be staring down at his feet in some silent and defeated contemplation. The hill was otherwise barren, snow rising to an unbroken ridge that served as a soft delineation between sky and earth.

"Is that a person?"

Anna seemed to take a while to hear me. She very deliberately put down the scissors she was using and looked over at my page.

"I don't know how I missed that," she said.

"It's kind of a distraction."

"I don't know how I missed it."

The despair in her voice scared me. "It's not a problem," I said. I had an inspiration and went into the front office to grab a bottle of Wite-Out, a kind of liquid eraser popular when people still typed on paper. Anna was staring at the person in the snow when I returned. I pulled the brush out of the bottle and dabbed a stroke of white across the figure, causing it to disappear into the hillside. I glanced over in triumph, expecting her to be smiling at my cleverness, but she was frozen with her hand halfway to the page.

"You shouldn't . . ." she began, and then returned to her

light table. A minute later she turned to me. "I could have printed another shot." Her voice was oddly breathless. "You didn't have to do that."

"But it was easy," I said. "It was no problem."

"But it wasn't . . ." She was trying to compose herself. "I had better shots. You can't just erase people."

"Okay . . . well . . . I'm sorry, but I don't see why it's such a big deal."

She shook her head and turned away.

"I know you don't."

"Hey . . ."

"Just leave it, Eric. *Please*."

For the rest of the night we worked in the cavernous back room in near-silence, passing strips of copy to each other from the waxer, sharing border tape and the one pair of sharp scissors, our carefully polite voices sounding overly loud when we had to speak.

. . .

I NEVER SAW HER ANYMORE outside of work, except from a distance on Main Street a couple of times as she shepherded her children from one store to another in the twilight. I had a sense she was spending a lot of time with her kids. They often appeared in the front office at the end of the day, waiting for her to take them one place or another, both unusually quiet, even Samantha, as if the winter had wrapped a woolen muffler around their exuberance. But I suppose they knew well by then what the season did to their mother. I'm sure they knew, because it was impossible not to feel the sadness that surrounded

Anna. Impossible not to feel it, and impossible in your weaker moments not to surrender to it as a kind of sleeping sickness that settled over the office sometimes late in the afternoon, when the light was already leaching out of the day, and each visitor brought a gust of cold air through the door and an awkward silence before they spoke in the hushed room.

In the midst of this late December gloom, Louise appeared by the side of my desk to announce that she had entered several of our stories and a couple of photographs in the state newspaper association awards, which would be announced the following February. She seemed to think this was good news, certain to brighten my day, and so I tried to respond the same way.

"That's great," I said. "Have we done this before?"

"Oh, we do it every year." She waved her hand to encompass the paper's long and, I thought, clearly triumphant past.

"Great. How many did we win last year?"

"Oh, none," Louise said cheerfully. "We haven't won anything for five years, at least."

I became aware that my proud smile no longer made any sense, and I was trying to figure out how to remove it and what exactly should go in its place as she patted me on my shoulder and strolled out the door.

. . .

CHRISTMAS AT HOME was the first without my father, but it was astonishing how present he was, how he appeared, quiet and expectant, in every awkward silence, how he took his empty seat at dinner, sitting in inscrutable, possibly forgiving judgment, how he sat in his spot on the couch on Christmas morning and watched us open our presents, waiting to see if we liked what we had been given. For years our presents from our parents had said, *From Mom and Dad*, on the tag, and this year they simply had our names on them and we all understood, of course, but holding the brightly wrapped packages in our hands it was as if our family had disappeared as a recognized entity. My brother and sister both held theirs too long before they tore the paper with false smiles, consecrating this new reality. I tugged a sweater from its wrappings, and as I held it up with my own hollow smile, I felt my father, who had been standing at the far end of the room with his arms crossed, back into the hallway and disappear. He had lingered to see us through this last loss. Now we were on our own.

I left two days after Christmas and drove across the gray, somnolent expanse of North Dakota. Shannon was as quiet as the snow-draped fields, Main Street deserted, drifts of snow gathered in the doorways. I was sitting in the chair in my living room, considering the scrim of ice along the bottom of the window, when I realized it was Sunday. Darkness climbed the glass, the broken coastline of ice inching up behind it, until I couldn't sit still any longer.

The night was the coldest so far, well below freezing. I hurried to my car and drove aimlessly, passing the deserted newspaper building twice before I saw Anna there, alone at her desk in the sallow illumination of the half-lit office, perfectly framed in the rectangle of the window against the blackness of the clouded night.

She never saw me approaching and was startled when the door swung open. I stood for a second on the far side of the counter, unable to move until the warmth had penetrated my skin. Anna sat frozen with her hands flat on top of her desk.

"Where are your kids?" I asked.

"At a birthday party."

"Lousy to have a birthday this close to Christmas."

She was silent a little too long, as if processing what I'd said took unusual effort.

"Why?"

"Anticlimax. Maybe just one set of presents."

She nodded, turned back to the typewritten pages in front of her.

"What are you doing here?" I asked.

Her voice was barely audible. "Trying to catch up."

The feebleness of this was too much. We weren't behind. Edith and I had taken care of it. There was no reason for her to be here. I shrugged off my coat and hung it on the rack, crossed the corner of the counter, and, before she could move, bent over her desk to consider the copy she was staring at blindly. I assumed my editor's voice, which I thought gave me the right to look.

"What are you working on?"

A single-page typewritten letter sat on her desk. An application for a job as the lifestyles reporter at *The Bemidji Herald*, some two or three hundred miles away across the border in Minnesota. She had made a couple of small editing changes in red ink, replacing a *which* with a *that* and changing *exiting opportunity* to *exciting opportunity*.

"That second mistake seems blatantly Freudian," I said, because Shannon had disappeared around me and I had no idea what to say.

Anna was silent.

"I don't know what's going on. But for God's sake, don't leave."

She turned her chair slowly, picked up the letter, tugged her coat off the rack, and walked out the door without bothering to put it on.

I had done something terribly wrong, but I didn't know what it was. Getting her to attend the wedding wasn't enough, not for the way her eyes had filled with despair as she raised them from the page. I was supposed to understand something that was escaping me. Yes, a terrible marriage once, I got that. Maybe I couldn't really know what it meant, but I got it.

There was something more. I sat at her desk and stared out the window, trying to pull into focus whatever was supposed to be in front of me, but all I saw was the deserted street and the blurred sentinel of a fir tree standing in its cloak of gray snow.

. . .

ANNA CALLED IN THE NEXT MORNING and said she wouldn't be in till late in the afternoon, at the earliest. It struck me that I would be on my way to the chamber of commerce meeting by then and out of the office. I thought about calling her, but she was claiming to be sick. There really wasn't much to do anyway. At noon I went to the café for lunch, wanting to be alone, but forced to deal with a slow stream of people who stopped by my table to tell me about this news or that or comment on this story or that. I was part of the community now. Halfway through my beer cheese soup served with popcorn instead of crackers, the house specialty since the day I had arrived, I set my spoon down, left money on the table, and walked out the door.

The wind was coming up and scattered flakes slanted out of a sky perched just above the rooftops. It was a lousy day for a walk, but I turned my collar up and headed toward the city park. Brown brick and dull glass on Main Street, then houses, isolated and smaller, islands braced against a frozen sea. Cars passed but no one else was stupid enough to be out strolling. I reached the park without realizing I had come that far and stared at the swings, each chain encased in a chrysalis of ice, faint reflections of blue and green visible in the indeterminate light. The town felt both overly familiar and strange. I was acutely aware of my presence in this one moment in time, which I felt as a moving, three-dimensional reality, a kaleidoscope rushing past while I stood motionless in the middle of it all. The sensation was peaceful and yet dissociative, as if the whirlwind had nothing to do with me, as if I'd ended up here completely by accident, opening my eyes to find myself standing in this park with its features erased by snow. My one concrete thought was wondering if I would remember this moment, which felt both vivid and already distant, later when it really *was* distant, when I had moved on to some future I could not yet conceive.

I have.

It seems odd, given all that would soon happen, the kind of event that usually frames itself, claims its permanent space in your memory by clearing away everything immediately before and after. But I understand why I can still see the ice on those chains, still remember the sense of numbness rising in my cheeks, the broken field of snow, the gray reef of sky. I can remember it all because I had run up against the receding edge of my life. I truly had no idea what came next.

. . .

THE PHONE RANG in the office at three-fifteen p.m. I was gathering up a notebook and pens, preparing to leave for the chamber meeting, when Edith took the call. She listened for a moment and handed the phone to me without saying a word. The deputy sheriff was on the other end of the line. A school bus returning from a field trip had been in an accident a few miles outside of town. He was heading out and could stop by and pick me up.

I sat in the front of the car. The heater was on full-blast and it was too warm. The moment we left the sheltering confines of town, snow blew hard across the highway, arriving out of the clouded world on one side of our headlights and disappearing into the nothingness on the other. The deputy drove too fast, pushing us forward into a tumbling tunnel of snowflakes like sparks in the light. I looked away from the road to control my nausea and as my eyes adjusted I saw the ghostly terrain of the barren fields dissolving within a few hundred yards, as if the world were burning away at the edges.

"Dwight's coming over from Wheaton," the deputy said, referring to his boss, the sheriff. "He should get there first."

He'd already told me the little he knew. An accident with a school bus. A vehicle overturned on a narrow county highway. He kept his eyes on the road but there was a tremor in his voice. I looked at his profile, the comically strong chin, slightly too long nose and forehead, a face of carved angles and planes interrupted only by his gentle eyes and absurdly long and feminine eyelashes. I realized he wasn't much older than I was, and he might well have gone to the local school.

He almost missed the turn and had to brake hard. I waited for the patch of ice that would add us to the accident list, but the car fishtailed into the narrow county highway and he accelerated again. "Icy," the deputy said, and I felt him lift his foot off the accelerator. We had the wind at our back now; you could see farther ahead. The road was as straight as a road in a dream, seeming to rise slightly as it disappeared into the sky. The bus appeared first, a yellow smudge in the white, becoming a lozenge the color of an old lemon and then clearly a bus, sitting upright, seeming to float in the middle of nothingness, but on its wheels on the side of the road. The deputy had slowed even more as soon as we saw it, and now he approached cautiously, as if some trap had been set. I couldn't see the sheriff's car, or anything else, but my eyes caught something black in the ditch, and beside it the eroded, wavering stick figure of a man clutching his hat.

"There's something in the ditch."

As we pulled over we saw the corner of the sheriff's car parked behind the bus. The deputy left his car running, gave me a brief, confused look, and opened his door. The wind bit my face as I stepped out on the other side of the car. The bus was only a few yards ahead, young faces pressed against the dark glass as if peering up from underwater. The deputy was already sliding down into the ditch toward the sheriff and the black object, which I could see now was an overturned vehicle, possibly a Jeep. I skated across the asphalt, which had a fine, nearly invisible scrim of ice, crossing the front of the bus to the door, which opened as I reached it. The driver was perched above, still in his seat.

"Are you all right?" I shouted. "Is everyone all right?"

He looked down at me, his eyes wide in shock.

"The back end's all messed up. I can't move."

"The bus?"

He seemed to consider this for too long. "Yes. The back end. Something's wrong."

"But the kids? Is everyone all right?" I stepped into the bus as I spoke, rising out of the door well into the long, cold interior, thirty or forty pale faces staring at me in unison.

"Are you all right?" I was still shouting, although it was oddly quiet inside the bus, the wind a flat, distant moan.

There were scattered, hesitant nods, a few murmurs of assent. Stephen, Anna's son, was sitting halfway down the bus on the left.

"Stephen. Is everyone all right? Is anyone hurt?"

He seemed embarrassed at being discovered.

"A few kids got knocked over. Jimmy's got a bloody lip. Lisa hurt her arm."

"I'm okay," a girl's voice said from the back.

"We got knocked down! Some kids were in the aisle. They shouldn't have been standing but they were and they got knocked down!"

It was a girl I didn't know, wearing a multicolored stocking cap over her pale yellow hair and standing as if she had been called on at school. Weak protests rose at being ratted out for standing.

"But nobody's hurt too bad?"

Head shakes now and louder reassurances.

"What happened?" I asked the driver. He stared at me. There was something wrong with him. "Everything's going to be all right," I announced uselessly to the rows of quiet children. "I'm going to go talk to the sheriff."

The blowing snow was pulsing red and blue on the highway. I crossed the front of the bus to see that an ambulance had pulled past and two paramedics, nearly invisible in their white jackets, were hurrying into the ditch. I followed them, taking short, careful steps along the glazed surface of the road, feeling the wind push at my back. The rear left quarter panel of the bus had been smashed in and the wheel was canted drunkenly inward. The black bumper trailed in the snow.

I was about to descend into the ditch when the EMTs reappeared out of a gust of blowing snow, inching uphill with a stretcher. I slid down a few feet to help. A dark-haired young woman, hair clotted with flakes, skin pale and wet, stared up at me as if I had dropped from heaven. She was blinking rapidly and I could see the skin in the small declivity where her throat met her breastbone moving in short, quick breaths. I had taken ahold of the stretcher right near her head and her eyes fixed on me as I helped them steady the stretcher on the asphalt.

"We got it. Thanks."

They slid her into the blackness of the open ambulance. I nearly fell as I slipped back down into the ditch, where the deputy knelt by someone stretched on the ground beside the Jeep, which lay on its side collecting snow. It was quieter down here. The snowflakes turned and danced in strange pockets and eddies of air. "Just a minute, now. Just a minute," I heard the deputy say. I could feel the stretcher-bearers coming down behind me. They were quick, but when they reached beneath the young man to slide him onto the stretcher he groaned. "Oh, Jesus," one of them said, pulling his hand away and staring at his glove covered with blood. "Farther down his back." They reached into the snow beneath him, exploring carefully. He groaned louder and shouted something I couldn't understand. Their eyes met and they lifted him quickly onto the stretcher as he screamed, "*Linda!*" The deputy helped them carry the stretcher up the slope.

The sheriff stood at the back of the Jeep, hands tucked into the pockets of his black nylon jacket, cap pulled low over his graying hair. He considered the interior of the vehicle, the space behind the seat open to the air and filled with a jumble of things my mind couldn't sort out. He crossed to the side, looking carefully at the snow, speaking absently, figuring it out for himself.

"The storm was worse. They come barreling down the road. They can't see fifteen feet ahead and they run into the back of the school bus. They don't hit it straight on. Maybe he jerks the wheel at the last minute. They hit it sideways and knock themselves into the ditch." He gestured back into the tumbled whiteness. "They turn over once. They don't have their seat belts on, of course. She's ejected from the vehicle. He goes up into the steering wheel, but probably would have been all right . . ."

The sheriff knelt and reached into the snow where several, small perfect holes were ringed with a tracery of pink.

" . . . except he had a toolbox in the back and it flies open . . ."

He pulled a screwdriver out of a hole in the snow, the metal point slick and wet and gleaming but still holding red flecks of flesh.

"... and these tools come flying out and nail him right in the back. Like a bunch of arrows."

He reached into another hole, a gash, and pulled out a chisel, sharp-edged, the handle stained black.

"What are the odds of *that*? Bad luck."

He considered the spot where the driver had fallen into the snow, a few feet ahead of us.

"Do you think he pulled them out himself? ... Jesus ..."

I could picture everything he had described. It was all very clear and easy to see, and I didn't want to see any of it so I looked up at the road. The ambulance was gone. I had missed it leaving somehow. The storm seemed to be abating. There was a faint sense of definition along the horizon.

"There's something wrong with the driver. In the bus."

The sheriff looked up from his contemplation of the chisel.

"He's not right. There's something wrong with him. You need to get him to a hospital."

Staring into the blankness of the storm, I saw something at the far edge of the world. Moving too fast. I slid up the ditch to get a closer look. Behind me the sheriff raised his voice.

"There's a tow truck coming. And another bus for the kids."

I was on the road and I could see it now. Not a tow truck. A battered green car. Coming too fast. A car I knew. I didn't realize what I was doing at first, but I started to skate down the road toward it. Raising my arms to be seen. Then I was running, slipping with each step, trying to close the distance before she got too close. I could see her sliding into the ditch or, worse, into the bus. Behind me I heard shouting—the deputy's voice—but I was in the middle of the road now, waving my arms wildly. With each ragged breath I pushed a cloud of white into the world and I was temporarily blinded, unable to measure the shrinking distance between us, so when I could see again, it was as if the car had jumped forward, and I could make her out now, hunched over the wheel. She wasn't going to be able to stop. My soul fled my body and I saw everything as I rose into the air. I saw the highway, ever so faintly glittering in its skin of ice, a gray line surrounded by white fields beneath a white sky, snow like brief erasures of reality falling across my vision. I saw the police cars behind me, the bright yellow school bus with ghostly faces floating in the dark windows, the upturned Jeep like a black tear in the day. My sight was so perfect I could see the blood creeping outward and thinning in its capillary action through the snow, each hole a tiny drain through which this universe would eventually collapse.

Anna's Buick slid sideways to a stop fifteen feet in front of me, the nose dipping into the ditch, but the rear end clinging to the road. She slipped on the ice as she stepped out, pulling herself back to her feet awkwardly. I was halfway to her by then.

"They're okay! They're all okay!"

She had gone deaf and tried to push past me, slipping again and falling into my arms. We sat down hard on the road, a ridiculous tableau, Anna pushing against my shoulder as I repeated the same words over and over and she seemed unable to hear me. "Not again!" she shouted. "*Not again!*" She swung her arm wildly, hitting me as hard as she could just beneath my right cheekbone, and as I recoiled she tried to pull herself to her feet to reach the bus and I thought of Stephen and how he would feel, and I held on to her arm and she fell backward again. Her car was on the left side of the road, and I didn't think the kids could see us, unless they had all crowded into the front. I thought there was still a chance this moment could not exist outside the two of us, if we kept it right here, if we held it close enough. I got a better hold of her arm and yanked hard, pulling her close, wrapping my arms around her. I pressed my lips into her ear.

"Stephen's okay. I talked to him. He's fine."

She shoved hard against my chest one last time.

"Anna, he's fine! They're all okay!"

"You're shouting," she said. "You're shouting in my ear."

I let go of her and she slid sideways on the cold asphalt. I turned so we were sitting side by side, facing the front of the bus down the road. The driver, still at his post behind the wheel, was faintly visible through the window.

"Not again?" I said.

Chapter 26

THEY WERE DRINKING TOGETHER and it made them happy, or it made him happy, and that made her happy—or happier, anyway. She sometimes felt, in the painful clarity of morning, lying dry-mouthed in bed while he slept soundly beside her, knowing she had to get up to start his breakfast and attend to their child, that she wasn't seeing it right, that she was mistaking something for something else, as if she had misunderstood a key word in a definition or lost track of a concept she once knew. But she pushed herself out of their disordered bed and into each day because there were chores to be tended to and they were happy. They were making it work.

The winter was a bad one, endless and raw, working its way through every crack in their tin box of a home. They were trapped indoors for days at a time. It was hard for all of them, but they were making it work. He hadn't hit her in a long enough time that she no longer flinched when he moved suddenly toward her. And he moved toward her a lot. He seemed consumed by a restless, furtive lust. The worst storm of the year blew in. His work shut down and it was impossible to get out of their tiny valley. By the second day the child was bouncing off the walls, tugging at doors, climbing headfirst over the tops of furniture. Anna remembered the striped blue shirt, saggy secondhand overalls, and mop of tousled, still-fine, sand-colored hair that always seemed to be scrambling around a corner, just escaping her grasp. By the third day she felt the trailer shrinking as rock-hard drifts rose around it. Her husband had ventured into the storm twice, once to check the car and another time because he worried the insulated pipes under the trailer might be freezing—both just excuses, really, to escape briefly into the wild air and snow-blind world.

The wind came around the front door and they had to push hard to get it latched when he returned. The storm door was loose and banged endlessly in the wind. Her husband, still in his heavy boots and sweater, sat at the small Formica table in the kitchen sipping coffee while snow melted out of his hair. The wall of white outside the window was turning an ashen gray that signaled the retreat of the day. She could see how hard he was trying, and it terrified her.

"Let's have a blizzard party," he said.

He made a special drink he had been served down home in Tennessee. It was so sweet, she thought she might gag, but he poured more sugar into his own glass and his smile was wide and eager and desperate and they drank more, straight bourbon now, and the country-western singer on the record he had chosen was singing about a swimming hole and it suddenly seemed funny, and when she laughed, she felt a glow settle over her and she thought this was all right, this was a good idea, after all, this was something to do. "Tell me what you'd do if you had a million dollars," he said, and Anna was speechless confronting the collapse of her own imagination. She had no idea. She could barely imagine what she would do with a hundred dollars. But when she shook her head, laughing helplessly, he was off, talking fast. It started with cars and went on to the very biggest Sony Trinitron television and a stereo system capable of waking the dead two states in every direction, and then he was learning how to play a Gibson electric guitar and there was something about NASCAR and a king-sized bed and a house on a lake with a powerboat. The room was rocking back and forth with his words, and she felt her heart rise at the size of his dreams and their impossibility. A million dollars had already been spent, but it was exhilarating to hear him go on and on, even if it seemed to her obscurely that it had stopped making sense some time ago, that it had simply become a list of things. She had so given up on the possibility of the world outside her sight that it left her dizzy and breathless to hear it piling up in all its riches in their tiny kitchen.

He ran out of words, staggered to the door, threw it open, and shouted, *Bring it on!* into the storm before he put on AC/DC, music she always hated, and he swung her into his arms to dance, although how you danced to this she wasn't sure; it didn't matter, the room was dancing, swinging wildly around her now and shifting colors as she hung helplessly on his shoulders and then they were in bed, and it was a tumult, and she reached for him desperately, threw herself at him because it was all she could do to keep from slipping into the blackness rising out of the corners of the bedroom, that swallowed her as soon as they were still.

She awoke hours later, feeling the room was colder than it should be. The storm door banged like a drunk pounding unevenly on a snare drum, each blow landing directly on her left temple. She staggered into the bathroom and was sick. She avoided her reflection in the mirror and stumbled back toward the bed, shivering uncontrollably. The wind seemed to be sweeping through the walls. She stopped beside the bed, hugging herself against the cold. Something wasn't right. There was something wrong.

She threw herself toward their child's room, hitting their closed bedroom door first with her shoulder, wrenching the latch out of the frame and knocking it into the wall as she fell into the hall. The wind sweeping through the trailer hit her and she saw the open front door in her mind, saw it clearly, a perfect rectangle opening into darkness, even before she slid on her knees into the kitchen and saw it waiting for her, not wide open, but ajar, the broken static of the storm reflecting the outside light above the entrance, the snow reaching across the linoleum like an encroaching flood, the narrow space through which frozen air rushed opening into the rest of her life.

. . .

"SHE MADE IT ABOUT FIFTY YARDS," Anna said. "She was walking in the direction of the stream. The snow had covered her and we didn't find her until the morning."

We were sitting in her car outside her house. We had been sitting there for some time.

"She? But your son is your oldest . . ." I stopped.

"Stephen is my second child. I got pregnant again sometime during that storm. Maybe that night."

Her second child. Not her first. Her second. I couldn't think of a thing to say. We sat there for a while, the heater rattling, snow still falling outside.

"What happened to your husband?"

"There was an investigation. I wanted them to throw us in jail. I hoped they would," she said with a sudden fierceness. "But they didn't. And then he left. Back down South."

I shook my head and, after a time, another question occurred to me.

"But Sam . . ."

Anna's smile was fleeting. "A man I met on a bus."

"Right."

She said nothing.

"Really?"

"On a bus from Dickinson to Seattle. Have you ever had something you wanted to do forever? Some silly thing? When I was a little girl we went to Dickinson to do some Christmas shopping. It was a big trip for us, and we passed the Greyhound station and there was a bus with those end-of-the-line glowing letters up above the front window. *Seattle*. And I thought, what would it be like to ride the bus all the way across Montana and through the mountains and to the sea? And it was something I always wanted to do after that."

"Okay. But . . . the man?"

"We were living with my parents." She stared through the window and the tumbling snow at her little house. "I was living with my parents again and I told them I wanted to go on a trip. They were just glad I wanted to do anything. They took care of Stephen. I took the bus out and I stayed in a hotel near the water for two nights and then I came home. He sat across from me on the way back. I can't explain it, but I knew if I slept with him I would get pregnant and I would have a girl. And I knew something else just as good . . ."

"What was that?"

"I'd never, ever see him again."

I had driven her home in her car, but she had her hands flat on the dash in the passenger seat, as if we were still flying down the highway a hundred miles an hour. I could see clearly the rings of pale, scarred flesh around each wrist. She saw me looking at them but made no effort to tug her sleeves forward.

"I had my little girl. I had my little girl. I knew I would and I did. I never thought she'd be the same and she wasn't. She isn't. But I had my little girl."

I stared out the window. After a while I heard Anna shift, felt her staring at me, and when I glanced over, her eyes were filled with tenderness. "There's a little time before the kids get home," she said. "I want to go down to the school and meet them. Thank you for stopping me from getting on the bus, Eric. Come in for a cup of coffee. I'll tell you the rest." She held up her wrists, as if they were in handcuffs. "I'll tell you about this."

Chapter 27

I REALIZED THAT NIGHT THAT I HADN'T interviewed the kids on the bus, and the next day I went over to the school at the end of the day and caught a couple of them to hear how they saw it happen. If Stephen saw his mom on the road that day he never mentioned it. We stood on the sidewalk in front of the school while he answered my questions and I found I was overly friendly, trying too hard. There was something in his manner, a way he watched me with a combination of uncertainty and caution, his thin lips held tight on his long, pale face, his feathery hair sticking out warily from beneath his stocking cap. We only spoke for a few minutes before I let him escape, running in his rubber-booted, gangly gait back to his friends.

The driver of the Jeep and his girlfriend were let out of the hospital within a couple of days, cut and badly bruised, but otherwise intact. The bus driver turned out to be hurt the worst. He'd injured his neck when the collision occurred and suffered from a lingering concussion the doctors didn't quite understand, but that left him disabled for the rest of my days in Shannon.

Anna was at her desk the next morning and in the look she gave me as I came through the door nothing was hidden; there was no regret, no retreat from the day before. We went back to our work. Now sometimes there were long periods of silence between us when we finished the paper together at night, but it was different, a kind of intimacy we didn't need to fill with words. Anything I might say about the passing spectacle of current events, about which I had once made endless pronouncements, now struck me as idiotic. One of the lesser gifts Anna left me was the sense not to take my own conclusions too seriously. I still talk too much, but I really understand if you're not listening.

The closest friend, I learned those last few weeks, is someone you share the unsaid things with. Not that we had become a pair of sphinxes. It's possible Anna spoke more than she had in the past, mostly about her children. Stephen's overly diligent sense of responsibility. The Man of the House, of course. The night terrors that left him covered in sweat and unable to speak, still caught in the nightmare even after the lights came on. His fondness for military histories, the sweeping martial epics of the ages. How she thought maybe he'd become a historian, prayed he would never become a soldier.

And then Sam, the girl conceived in a motel in Red Lodge, Montana, how much her fearlessness scared her mother, how much it reminded Anna of Katy, her first child. When Anna told me these things she spoke calmly with a subdued sense of relief, as if it was good to be able to say them aloud. The only time she choked up was when she said the name of her first child. She only said it once. For the rest of that night she said hardly anything, and I understood that Sam had been her bid to keep going, but that the price had been something she hadn't understood at the time, an inability to ever completely shut the door, not a ghost, but something worse, a sister, alive and determined to make her own mistakes. "I let them go out, you know," Anna said as we locked up that night. "I let them go out with their friends and by themselves to play and it scares me every time. Sam scares me so much, but I let them go out."

I told her about my brother and sister and how they were struggling after my father's death, and the practical advice she gave me made me feel even younger than I was, and made me doubt I would ever be capable of being an actual parent. We also talked about lesser things, able now to share our opinions of Art and Louise and other people we had come to care about with a new candor, knowing it wouldn't be misunderstood for cruelty. One thing we never talked about was the letter I caught her writing to *The Bemidji Herald*. We both knew it hadn't been sent.

We finished early one Thursday evening, and while we were waiting for Paul to show up, Anna wandered off to the big press, the one they ran the paper on. It filled up a third of the room, a mad-scientist creation of rollers and gears and moving parts you could lose yourself in. She ran her hands through her thick hair, pushing it off her shoulders, and I remember the way she let her sleeves fall without thinking about it and how I fought off an impulse to hug her.

"Did you ever think about how amazing this really is?"

"I'm always amazed when they can get the damn thing to work," I said.

Anna kicked the side of my foot.

"I mean the whole thing. We go out. We take a few pictures—a pretty baby, a thunderstorm above the lake. We talk to a few people, ask some questions, and then we put it into these little stories, we write a few cutlines. And then in just a few hours it ends up on these pages and it goes all over town and people actually *read* it. They look at the pictures and we make them happy or sad—"

"Or they wonder why we're wasting their time," I said, "or they don't care at all."

This time she pushed gently against my arm with her fist.

"But they do. That's what I'm saying. They *do*. Don't you ever think how amazing that is? We were sitting at our desks and I was worrying about the kids or the electric bill, and you—well, who *knows* what you're thinking, Eric?—but we have all these things floating around in our heads and we push them aside and we put down these words. We type and some paper spins around on this thing and there they are. Forever."

"Or until they're used to line the trash."

Anna shook her head. "Or until they're put away in the attic for the grandkids. Or until they're filed in the city library. They're there. We're really *lucky*." She said the word as if she could not quite believe it, and then she spun on a heel to face me. "You do know what I mean. And you think it's amazing, too."

"Sure."

And before I knew what I was doing I kissed her on the temple. Because at that moment we knew we shared a secret: newspapers, which pretended to be the most transitory of media, were really forever. We were part of an eternal narrative that stretched back to Gutenberg and on into the infinite future. We were certain that their cheap, broadsheet record of our world would be with us always. Nothing could take their place.

Years later I look back on that day and find it framed by the recent memory of the newspaper chain I worked for being sold off in pieces like the estate of some deceased dowager, several of the papers shuttered, others surviving in ghostly half-lives as appendages to websites that serve as glorified billboards. The idea that the past promises us a certain future is always an illusion, of course, but to see the substance of our world slipping out of existence would have been unimaginable to Anna and me then, and so it strikes me this story is, in some lesser part, also a record of a time when words were physical things, immutable once they were stamped into paper, and a small newspaper could believe it mattered, was providing a record for the community it served—flawed, inadequate, but as permanent in its own way as parchment inked by monks bent over their copy boards a thousand years earlier.

. . .

IN LATE FEBRUARY Louise burst into the newsroom, looking more drunk than was usual at noon.

"We won!" she announced, teetering as she spread her arms to take in an adoring crowd.

A brief, confused silence. "Won what?" Edith asked, without bothering to look up from the copy she was editing.

"The state press association awards! We won three first-place prizes!"

And we had. Our flood coverage had won the overall award for community service, which was the big one. A photograph taken by Anna of exhausted workers toiling in the dark at the dikes beneath the floodlights had won best spot news photography. Three linked stories about the county commission's struggles to adjust the mill levy for badly needed highway repairs, which I'd considered quite possibly lethally boring when I'd written them, had even won the award for best investigative series.

Louise broke out the bottle of blackberry brandy from Art's office and we were drinking a toast in paper cups when Anna surprised us all.

"I'm going to hold a party," she said. "To celebrate."

. . .

IT WAS A NICE PARTY. Anna bought pinwheels and party hats for all the kids and they careened through the house making helicopter noises. Willie Nelson was singing a bit too loudly about a redheaded stranger and there was mulled wine, thick with fruit and nuts. "It's called glogg. I'm Swedish, you know," Anna announced with mock gravity when I looked into my glass with eyebrows raised.

"Uh-huh."

"Oh, yes," she said with the same deadpan. "My mother's sister married a man from Oslo."

"That's Norway."

"Just drink," said Todd, who had been listening with his arm around Christina. "You won't care."

I did and I didn't, and the mulled wine definitely helped

when we gathered in the living room for the toasts by Art and Louise, his overly brief and hers too long, but at least free of French quotations. Todd led a hearty cheer when Art held up our three first-place certificates, just paper, really, but embossed with gold foil and words written in formal dark blue calligraphy. The kids, piled onto the couch, blew their noisemakers, Stephen blowing his very seriously, as if auditioning for a place in a band, Sam shaking her head sideways with pure joy, her red curls bouncing side to side as she blew so hard she slid backward off the couch and landed at my feet, looking up at me with hair in a tangle and her eyes wild and wide. "Mr. Eric!" she shouted, and blew her horn at my knees.

It was all silly and loud and perfect—I still remember that moment as perfect—the squeaky but exhilarated fanfare of plastic whistles proclaiming the unlikely triumph of *The Shannon Sentinel.*

When the official celebration broke up, I retreated into the short hall that led to the bedrooms. I had been smiling for an hour and I wanted a moment to myself. I reached the slightly ajar door to Anna's bedroom, which I could see had been carefully put in order, and before I really thought about what I was doing, I slipped inside.

It was a small room, lit only by a bedside reading lamp. At the center was a sagging, full-sized bed with a plain beige coverlet and an old brass headboard. A small circular table, the kind you can find at any discount store, sat on one side, and a bookcase on the other. I looked briefly at the books, but it was hard to make out the titles in the gloom. On the wall across from the bed stood a low dresser with a mirror. Pictures of her children sat in frames on top of the dresser, and there was another photo stuck in the side of the mirror at eye-height.

I considered it absently, feeling mildly guilty for prying, and then I had the oddest sensation, as if the world blinked out and then refocused, slipped into a brief, heart-stopping void, and then returned with surreal clarity. The music and voices drifting into the room disappeared. It was perfectly quiet. I tugged the picture out of the mirror frame and then I was standing beside the bed, holding it beneath the light. Looking at a picture of myself.

The photograph was in partial profile, a close-up taken outdoors on a day of scattered clouds. A moment drifted back: Anna and I sitting on the fake island by the lake, taking pictures of sailing boats. The camera clicking in my ear. And here it was. In her mirror. In her bedroom. I felt my own complete and overwhelming stupidity, my ignorance of every single thing that mattered in the last year of my life, and about the only thing I knew for sure was that you didn't put a picture there of someone who was just a good friend.

I put it back. When I stepped into the hall I was terrified she would be standing outside the door, but no one was, and I hurried through the living room and past the group in the kitchen, smiling, nodding, saying I needed to get a little air.

Out on the sidewalk I realized my coat was lying on the bed in Stephen's room. The night was cold but I couldn't go back in. I needed to get away from the street, where I felt nakedly visible, so I stepped around the side of the house. It was darker here, the snow-covered yard falling away into the dark ravine. I stood out of sight of the kitchen window, holding myself against the cold, trying to think. The door opened and shut with a rattle and I heard her walking up behind me.

"Eric? What are you doing?"

"I don't know."

Anna moved up to my side and when I looked at her I knew I was right about the photograph. She stood silently beside me for what felt like a long time.

"You know what you need to do now?" she asked.

"No."

"You need to go."

This was not what I expected.

"What?"

"You need to go. You need to leave Shannon. You've been here long enough. You're twenty-one years old. You need to move on."

The wind blew through our clothes and this was a lonely place, there was no debate. She stood the way I had seen her so many times, with her arms crossed across her chest, her over-long sleeves held in in the palms of her hands. She was pale and indistinct in the faint light behind her home, a sketch of a woman I realized I had never really known, and this only seemed to clarify her, the one knee bent slightly, the slight arch of her back, and the way she always held her head, as if an invisible book were perched there. She was drawn in these few lines and I had to fill in the rest. I felt like I was seeing her for the first time, and I knew how much she meant to me.

"Move on," I said.

"Come with me."

We walked down the ridge. Her house was the last one in

line and it didn't take long before we had left it behind. Shannon sparkled and glowed off to the south, but to the north and west the broad, enveloping darkness of the American plains brought the sky and earth together in a single black sheet, broken only by a handful of stars and a solitary farm light off in the distance.

"You know, sometimes I come out here at night after the kids are asleep, and I don't look at Shannon. I look out there," Anna said. "In the dark it seems like there's nothing between you and the rest of the world. Everything is out there. You need to get out there, Eric. You've done what you can with this little newspaper. You've done all you were meant to do here. You don't want to get stuck."

"What about you? You're the one who comes out here at night looking at the rest of the world."

Anna smiled, but her eyes never left the invisible distance.

"I'm just a romantic. This is my home. I'm happy here."

I was smart enough to know that was true and not true, but too young to realize it's the same for almost everyone at some point: we stop moving, we come to the end of the search, yet some part of us forever inclines toward the horizon, the way you feel your legs still moving after a long day on your feet, some restless phantom wants to go on, even if we have made a home. I write that with a wife I love asleep down the hall, but Anna was alone, except for her children. I have a daughter, I know how much that is. I also know it's not the end of desire.

"I don't believe it," I said. "I think it's just as small a place for you as it is for me. I think you could go somewhere else." I hesitated, and amid a confused rush of longing I barely heard myself say, "We could find work somewhere together."

She stepped close enough to place her hand flat against my chest. Her sleeve slid down, leaving her arm naked and exposed in the dark. I felt her palm against my heart.

"Oh, Eric. Here is what you're going to do. Next week you're going to tell the Shoemakers that you're quitting at the end of the month. You're going to go back to school and finish or you're going to find a job somewhere else. You've got experience, and you're impressive. You're an impressive young man." Her voice tapered off and she let her forehead touch my chest. Just briefly. "You are. So you're going to move on. If you don't, here's what I'm going to do. I'm going to edit an error into one of your stories so severe they'll have to fire you. And you'll have to leave Shannon, anyway."

She lifted her head so I could see her eyes and know she was serious. Then, gently at first, but with ever-growing firmness, she pushed herself away.

"Just don't tell me you did that to Stacy," I said.

"No, Stacy managed all by herself. No need for help there."

"I guess I'm not quite as capable."

"Well, you're young. You'll learn how to screw up soon enough." And I thought she might cry, but she managed one more smile. "But not today."

I tried one more time. "Listen—"

Anna turned toward her house. "Come on. We have to get back inside. You don't understand, do you? I'm throwing you a goodbye party."

Chapter 28

ART WAS DISTRESSED; LOUISE SEEMED flummoxed and then nodded firmly, as if it had been her idea all along. "You're ready to move on to a daily," she said. We were sitting in Art's office and there was really nothing more to say. The date had been set. But there was one more thing I had decided I was going to make happen.

"You need to make Anna editor," I said.

Art's hands came off the desk like startled birds. Louise's death-star eye fixed on a spot on the wall somewhere above my head.

"I don't know about that. It takes a certain kind of—"

"She can do it. She'll do it her own way—more . . . *quietly*. But she can do it."

Louise was shaking her head but I could see the possibility turning over in her mind.

"You know what I really appreciated about working here?" I said.

"That we had some *fun*?"

"Sure. That, too. What I appreciated was that you gave me a chance. I hadn't done this before and you were willing to give me a chance."

Art was holding the side of his head like he had a toothache. Louise's eye burned a hole through the wall directly above my head. Then she smiled, the way she did when she looked over my shoulder while I was writing and saw a turn of phrase she liked.

"I've been working with her for months," I said. "She can do the job. She won't ask for it. But she can do it."

"We'll see," she said. "I'll talk to her, Ricky."

"Give her a chance, Louise."

Now it was Art, unexpectedly, who spoke. He gestured outward to take in the entire human menagerie of the newspaper and the print shop on the other side of his wall.

"Surely, my boy, you've noticed we give *everyone* a chance around here."

. . .

ON A SUNDAY MORNING I drove out of Shannon for the last time, the backseat and the trunk filled with cardboard boxes. There had been an official going-away party, of course, and several "final" rounds at the Buffalo Bar. Todd had insisted on helping me pack, although it was sad how little I had really accumulated during my time in town, not one stick of furniture, a few albums and books of my own, a few more books and albums that Emily had left behind. A sturdy pair of winter boots. A white enamel whiskey bottle of Elvis. Too few photographs.

Todd and I sat amid the boxes, the day graying outside the window, and drank a final beer.

"You should come back and visit sometime," he said.

"Absolutely."

"You still don't have a job lined up?"

"Not yet, nope."

"You'll find something."

"How's married life?" I asked, because I thought it seemed good, but I wanted to know.

Todd cocked his head. "It's good. It's great, man. It beats ESPN. You should try it yourself sometime."

All the goodbyes, the usual promises, but, blessedly, no one around as I got into my loaded car and drove down Main Street one last time. The town was still asleep, and instead of heading straight out to the highway, I cruised the length of Main and then circled back, past the park, the high school, blocks of already familiar homes, and out to the edge of town by the Midwestern Forge factory. The two places I avoided were the office and Anna's home. I wanted to remember the office the way it had been on my last day, Edith working with her blunt red pencil at the front desk, Art in his office, Todd and Paul in back, the part-time women making themselves busy with typesetting and ad design.

Only Anna had been absent, finding an assignment that took her out of the office when it was time for me to leave. I understood, and it didn't change anything. In my mind she was there. I saw her at her desk in front of the big window, hands on the keyboard, wrists arched in the manner any typing teacher would applaud, chin high. Perfect posture. I had seen her like this out of the corner of my eye for months, a quiet reassurance tucked into nearly every day. Anna.

. . .

I TOOK OUT A MAIL SUBSCRIPTION to the *Sentinel*. It arrived in my mailbox in the Twin Cities nearly a week late. I was working in a copyediting job for a legal publishing firm and hating it. I leafed through every issue that came, reading the stories Anna liked enough to give herself a byline. I could hear her voice when I read them and it kept me company at night in my tiny apartment too near the squalor of Hennepin Avenue. I stayed at the publishing firm for six months before I got a job with the *Duluth News Tribune*, a mid-sized daily in a tough steel mill and port town perched on the frigid shore of Lake Superior. The city had everything a reporter could want: corrupt politicians, angry labor unions, seedy nightlife, occasional bloody mayhem down by the docks. I started out covering the county commission and got moved to the city council just in time for the scandal of the decade: the city planner had been taking paybacks from a local Indian tribe to deed them a block of city property that would allow them to build a casino in the heart of town.

I broke the story when his secretary, an honest woman from the Iron Range who hated him with generations of stored-up, working-class ire, slipped me an envelope with the check numbers and the bank account in North Dakota he had been using. (Only a Duluth political hack could mistake North Dakota for the Cayman Islands.) I wrote the story and my career was made.

I read the *Sentinel* diligently when I first moved to the Twin Cities, but I had less time for it in Duluth. The *News Tribune* was owned by the Knight-Ridder Corporation, which as I said has since been chopped up and devoured by corporate piranhas. At the time it was the second largest newspaper chain in the country. When a job in the Knight-Ridder Washington Bureau covering the senators and congressmen from the Upper Midwest came open, I applied and got the post. I moved to Washington, D.C., and the *Sentinel* subscription never made the journey. I was too busy to call and straighten it out, and when the subscription expired, I lost touch.

Anna and I never spoke after I left Shannon. She sent a postcard once from the state newspaper convention in Fargo on the day the paper won four awards. She tried to give me credit, but it was all her. I called her old number to offer congratulations, but when the machine picked up, I hung up. I don't really know why.

We never spoke, but she was part of so many things in those years after the *Sentinel*: the resolve that allowed me to get up and face every day at the legal publisher's without complaining; the determination that it wouldn't be where I ended up; the wisdom that it was better to be alone than to be with the wrong person, a lesson I learned imperfectly, but that at least gave me the sense to know what I had found when I met my wife. In all this, she was present.

The person I kept in touch with was Todd. He continued to pass on regular news of the local high school sports teams under some misapprehension that they had mattered to me. He never said much about himself, but he did send pictures of their first baby, and the second, and the third. I tried to picture him growing older, the ink stains ever darkening on his fingertips, but he was lodged in my head as the young man with the jumping Wile E. Coyote tattoo and the lawn-mower haircut.

Art Shoemaker died of a heart attack in his house one autumn afternoon, toppling over piles of newspapers that nearly completed the burial right then and there. Todd wrote me that the firemen had a hard time clearing a path to get the body out. Louise ran the shop and newspaper for another year and then sold both to Paul Strand, as I'd thought would eventually happen, and moved to Florida, where she had a sister. I tried and couldn't imagine her sitting contentedly on a beach. It didn't seem like she would be having nearly enough *fun*.

And I couldn't imagine her without Art. They now seemed so clearly joined by love.

Todd's communication over the years had all been by mail, not even email, but the old-fashioned kind that arrives in an envelope. It might have been because he could use the envelopes and the postage machine at the office and never had to pay for anything. I didn't recognize his voice, or even place his name at first, when he called to tell me Anna was dead.

"How did it happen?" I asked.

He told me, and a vision of Anna silhouetted in a darkened room, the bottle rising through the shadows, the very real weight of it in her small hand, the brief, deceptively cool feeling of the plastic against her lips, filled my head and then flared out as if I had been staring into the sun. The world burned away into a perfect blackness and blankness, an infinite emptiness. Todd's voice drifted up out of this void. ". . . *bleach*, man . . . it had to hurt like hell."

"Yes."

"I don't know about the motel, either," he said, "why she drove all the way across town like that."

Each word seemed to arrive out of the darkness with a strange clarity.

"She didn't want to leave the house haunted, for her kids, or whoever ended up living there," I said. "That's the kind of thing she would think of."

"Yeah. I suppose." He sounded doubtful. "It's terrible, man."

We spoke for only a few more minutes. He told me about the half-open door and the plans for the funeral, which was in a couple of days. I was leaving town that night for an assignment there was no way I could get out of, so I wouldn't be able to go. The thought was a small, shameful relief. I didn't want my final memory of Anna to be of her in a box.

After Todd and I had finished I tried to go back to work. It had been a lot of years and I had some misguided sense I should try to carry on. But I couldn't concentrate. So as I said at the beginning, I rode the elevator down to the bottom of the National Press Building, walked over to Lafayette Square, and took a seat on a bench.

The street was busy, the square filled with tourists and cubicle dwellers escaping briefly into the sun. The fact of Anna's suicide, the particulars of her death, settled on me, and I could hardly move. But mingled in the sorrow was a strange sense of dislocation, as if time had slipped out of order. How, I wondered, could this be now?

. . .

THE DAY OF THE BUS ACCIDENT, when we sat in her car and then went inside, Anna made me a cup of coffee and sat down beside me on her couch, and I remember I was somewhat surprised by this, how close she sat, but I never understood—what did I understand, really?—and she told me that four days after Katy had frozen to death, after the police had come and gone, after the social worker visits, after her husband had fled, and her broken parents had retreated to their farm, she found herself alone one evening in the trailer, vacantly packing their belongings. Every time she passed through the kitchen, the door called to her, a silent invitation, insinuating and knowing. Finally she saw there was no point in trying to resist. The door knew her secret. They wanted the same thing. She looked around the trailer for a length of rope, but there was none to be had. Then she had an inspiration. She took a kitchen knife and walked around the back of the house, where hay bales had been placed against the foundation to keep the wind from getting under the trailer. She sawed at the stubborn bailing twine and finally cut loose a long strand. She pulled hard on it. Sturdy enough. She put it in her pocket and walked back around to the front of the trailer.

The night was nothing like the storm, she said. Cold and clear. A quarter moon, but enough light reflecting off the snow to see. She followed the path she thought Katy must have taken, down the familiar route toward the creek, and then lost, veering off into the meadow. She came to the spot, what she thought was the spot in the dark, but there was nothing there, no way to hold herself, to make sure she couldn't escape her own judgment. The temptation was just to lie down, close her eyes where Katy had, but she was afraid she would change her mind, would find some reason for a pardon or simply surrender to her own weakness. She walked a few yards farther toward the creek and an idea came to her. An old threshing machine had been left behind generations ago, rusting and slowly sinking into the earth. A part of the machine, a long boom used to dump grain into trucks, still rose into the air. Anna tied the twine carefully and tightly around one wrist and then tossed a loop over the boom. She tied the other wrist. It was difficult above her head, but she repeated the knot until it was impossible to undo. The twine was stiff in the cold, but she was careful to do it properly. When she was finished wrapping her other wrist, she stood on her toes and slid the loop of twine higher up on the angled boom, until it was just below the spot she had noticed silhouetted against the moon, the spot where there was a notch in the metal. She stretched and jumped and the loop slid an inch higher and caught in the notch. She wasn't going anywhere now. She had fixed herself to the night and the growing cold. The twine cut into her wrists, but soon she couldn't feel it any longer. The cold was the same, very soon it went from something you felt to a concept, like the infinite distance revealed in the night sky. She could see back to the place where she believed they had found Katy, and over time the spot seemed to collect and hold the wintry light. The last thing she remembered was thinking she could see the faint impression of her daughter filled with stars.

"My dad cut me down at about three in the morning," Anna said. "He woke up in the middle of the night convinced I was going to do what I did and he drove back out to the trailer and found me. They thought I might lose the use of my left hand at first, but it hadn't been long enough. Then I had to stay in a hospital for a while until they were convinced I wouldn't go looking for more rope and another threshing machine." She fixed me with a weak smile. "So. That's the story behind the mystery of Anna's long sleeves. What do you think?"

What could I say?

"I think there aren't that many of them still around. Threshing machines. The odds you could find one in that condition again are probably insurmountable."

Anna leaned into my shoulder, laughing and maybe crying, and for the one and only time, gave me a fierce hug. I have said she was a small but not delicate woman, and yet at that moment she seemed so fragile, I hardly dared to put my arms around her.

• • •

HOW LONG HAD I BEEN sitting on the bench? The people in the square were all different and the sun had moved an odd distance across the sky. A child, a little girl, escaped her mother and ran into the pigeons farther down the path, where a bored middle-aged man had been tossing them scraps of his sandwich. They scattered into the air in a flurry of wings and ruffled feathers, gathering quickly and circling in a black and gray arc to land exactly where they had been. I was struck by a sense of time as fleeting and illusory as their flight, all the years a tight circle back to where we started. Could this really be the answer—all she had done, the children raised, the friends, the work, the good stories, the things she made her own, all of it too brief a turn through a sky filled with fading light?

The rest of the day was like sleepwalking. I marched

through it blankly, unable to think, unable to tell anyone, not even my wife. I caught my plane out of National Airport that evening, and I was looking down at an island of lights far below on some featureless Midwestern plain, when I remembered a summer night in Shannon. A bonfire on the edge of the lake, a distant shore nearly invisible in the darkness. A rowboat.

How did we come to be here? A drunken bet that Anna and I could beat Todd and Christina across the lake. Something to do with who would make the better pirates, a conversation started by Christina.

Anna and I were lousy pirates. Despite a hearty shout of, *Ahoy, matey*, and many an, *Avast, ye black'earts*, the other boat had coursed ahead into the inky blackness and soon we were rowing alone across the mirrored lake, the stars parting at our prow and rippling back into their proper constellations in our wake.

When we had both tried to row we had been unable to move in a straight line, and now I was idly pulling us in the general direction of the Big Dipper. Anna sat in the back of the boat, trailing a hand in the water. The party on the shore was still going strong and the music and occasional hoots of laughter reached us with crystalline clarity like the music in your head late at night, the voices of dreams, very close and yet far away, not quite real.

"Beautiful," Anna said, and I knew she was looking at the stars. I shipped the oars to rest and we glided along.

"The air's still so warm," she said. "I love it when the day hangs on like this."

"That's because you're not rowing."

"You're not rowing, either."

"That's true. I give up. They win."

"They win," she said lightly.

The party going on across the water was for the birthday of the owner of the café where Christina worked. I was only there because she had invited Todd and he wanted someone he knew along. Christina had invited Anna, whom she always felt needed more nights out, away from the kids.

"Christina wins," I said. "I think the whole pirate thing was just a way to get Todd alone in a boat."

"Oh, I think Todd won, too."

As Anna spoke, the bonfire on the side of the lake disappeared, as if slowly erased by an unseen hand. We were floating in perfect, moonless darkness.

"The party's gone."

I felt the boat shift as Anna looked over her shoulder.

"How does that happen?" I said.

"We must have gone around a point."

"Let's hope so."

"You're not rowing in a straight line."

"There are no straight lines. The universe is curved."

Anna's head went back, a barely seen shadow of falling hair as she contemplated the broad arch of stars.

"Yes, it is."

We drifted awhile longer, the music fading until it seemed imagined.

"I suppose we should head back," I said.

"No. Let's stay out here awhile longer."

A splash echoed in the silence and we both turned to see

a ripple in reflected stars a few feet from the boat. There was another, and another. The still water tangled now with concentric circles, and then the form of a fish half out of the water, barely, briefly there, and, once seen, another. We were both still, watching them feed.

Then they were gone.

Anna dropped her arm as deeply into the water as she could—I felt the boat shift—and lifted it high, the sound of water falling back into the lake etched clearly in the silence.

"What are you doing?"

"Trying to imagine what the sky looks like to a fish. Trying to see the stars through the water."

"Okay, then. Time to head back."

I picked up the oars again and made my first broad stroke in the water. We slid between stars above and below, and the feeling was like beginning a long, slow, effortless descent through the heavens.

"Eric." She leaned forward and splashed water my way. It fell short. She splashed harder and I felt it against my arm. "Eric, Eric, Eric. You would make a lousy fish."

"A lousy fish. A lousy pirate." I pulled on the oars. "I better get us home."

Anna leaned forward and held my hand, stopping me from rowing.

"Have you ever seen the ocean?"

"Sure," I said, surprised at the urgency, the strength in her small hand.

"Do you know I've never seen the ocean?"

"No."

"I have. I *have* seen the ocean, but not really. I saw it once in Seattle, but I never saw it. It was too early. I took a trip and saw the ocean, but I never really saw it. And now every day is another day I haven't seen the ocean. I think trying to see the stars through the water makes total sense. I think trying to be a fish makes *total* sense."

The boat rocked. We both became aware of her hand holding mine at the same time, and when she let it go, I felt the damp ring around my wrist as if it were filled with light, and it reminded me of everything I didn't understand about her.

"Hallucinations are common at sea," I said. "We'll get you home and you'll be fine."

She was still leaning forward, close, and I wasn't sure if I could really see her eyes, or maybe it was just the way her body was poised, but she seemed to be weighing something. The boat drifted on the mirror of the lake, and there was nothing else, nothing but the two of us inclined toward each other in this silent balance, until I heard her take a breath and she splashed in my direction, gently at first and then harder.

"Eric, Eric, Eric."

"What?"

"You should really try to be a fish."

She was still close and the water was hitting us both, and I could feel it against my face and I could see it in faint, fractured reflection on her cheeks. High above the world in an airplane, I knew she had done the right thing sending me on my way. I would not have changed the course of my life. And I understood my own hesitation, my own refusal to see some things until too late. We draw lines to protect the people most important to us.

This woman who claimed she was done with men, who carried her damage like a faint shadow across even the brightest day. This friend who had already placed so much of her trust in me. This woman briefly splashing water in my eyes. This friend I needed to prove I deserved. This beautiful woman. This friend.

But I wanted that moment back. I wanted to feel the water on her face, not just mine. I wanted to slide into the midnight lake together. I wanted to be a fish. I wanted to course weightless through the warm darkness with her and wrap our submerged bodies together and breathlessly stare at the blurred stars at the end. I knew how much it would have complicated our lives, and I wasn't foolish nor arrogant enough to think it would have necessarily saved her, but I wanted it so badly. I wanted it for myself, and more than anything, I wanted to show Anna it was possible.

Chapter 29

I WAS SURPRISED TWO YEARS LATER when I received an invitation to Stephen's wedding. He was living in Alexandria, only a few miles outside of Washington, and the wedding was at the Episcopal church in Old Town that had once been George Washington's church. I hesitated but finally decided to go. It was a bright spring morning. Stephen had grown into a tall, somewhat pensive-looking young man, with dirty blond hair and pale skin. He didn't look much like her at all.

I introduced myself in the receiving line.

"Thank you for coming. I think you were the last close friend my mother ever had," he said. There was an old question in his eyes, and I understood now why I had been invited.

"I was honored to be her friend," I said, pretending I didn't see it. "I didn't know you were in D.C. What are you doing here?"

"I work for Senator Dorgan. I have for a while. Legislative affairs."

"That's great. He's a good man."

"Yes, he is."

I was about to move on.

"I was a little jealous of you at the time, actually," Stephen said, still looking at me with a quiet, attentive curiosity that suddenly reminded me very much of her.

"Trust me. If you could see me back then, you'd know there was nothing to envy."

He shook his head, as if uncertain how to take that, and then laughed.

"Well, thank you for coming, Mr. Valery. Make sure you say hi to Sam."

But I didn't. I introduced myself to the very beautiful bride and her parents and I saw Sam up ahead, talking with vigorous animation to a couple her age. She still had her wild red curls and the same freckles, the same radiant, reckless energy, but she had grown into her mother's slight yet sturdy figure, and as she leaned forward to tell her friends something, it was as if I were seeing an alternate, untroubled version of Anna, the one who never married too soon, who never ended up on the floor of that trailer staring at a half-open door.

I slid out of line and worked my way around to the side of the church, where a handful of ancient gravestones tilted on the verdant lawn. I resisted the urge to walk over and study the inscriptions. It felt out of tune with the day. They turned out all right, Anna, I thought. You did good. They turned out well.

"Stephen said you were back here. What are you doing?"

Sam was teetering through the soft grass on high heels.

"Just taking a moment."

"My mom's last great love. You were too young for her, you know."

Well, there you were.

"Certainly too immature, anyway," I said. "Still."

"And odd. You did always seem a bit odd."

"Once again. Unchanged."

She was standing beside me now, and when I glanced at her in profile, it was too much. I looked at the graveyard.

"Cheery spot you've picked," Sam said. "It's a celebration, you know. My brother's marrying a nice girl with loads of money."

"You've grown up. You and Stephen both."

"Yep. Sorry. You kind of look the same, *Mr. Valery.*"

"Rick, please."

"Mom always called you Eric."

"I can't believe you remember that."

She hesitated. "I don't, really. Stephen does. I don't really remember you at all. Just this shadowy, big, very, *very* old man who was my mother's boss. Stephen remembers you. I remember your picture."

I looked at her then.

"It was a long time ago. I was twenty-one years old."

Sam seemed to take this as a mild rebuke. She shrugged.

"I just wanted to make sure you knew you were invited to the reception. It's at the Palmer House."

She started back to the church and then stopped and turned.

"She had a lot of happy years, you know. She loved being the editor of the paper. And you should have seen her the day

Stephen graduated from college. Her health was terrible then, everything hurt and they could never get the medication right, but you should have seen how happy she was."

Her tone was so familiar I couldn't help but smile. "You sound like her. She was always explaining things to me."

"She had a good life. For a long time she had a good life. That's all I'm trying to say. Just because—" Sam shook her head impatiently.

"Was there a note?" I heard myself ask.

And now Sam wished she hadn't stopped. "No. Everyone wants a note. Something that ties it up all real neatly. *Oh, this is why.*"

That was true, I was about to say. People want explanations.

"I just think she was tired," Sam said. "Everything hurt and I just think she was tired. She knew we could take care of ourselves. She said goodbye. I look back and I realize she was saying goodbye all the last weeks. She had this . . ."

She shook her head again, unhappy she couldn't find the word. I wondered how much she and her brother knew.

"Did she ever talk about the end of her marriage?"

Sam's green eyes—green, not the same color as her mother's at all—considered me with heightened doubt. "Just that it was hard. Raising a child. I knew I came along later. A boyfriend that didn't last." She smiled. "Hard to imagine."

"Not really. The boyfriend, I mean. Your mother was beautiful."

"She said Stephen's dad had disappeared and she knew it was hard, but we didn't want to know him, and she'd lost touch with the boyfriend. We used to wonder, of course. Stephen, particularly. But . . ."

So that was it. I couldn't imagine she would tell anyone else if she hadn't told her children. That I had been the one to whom her secret had fallen seemed a strange and precious honor, a faith I wasn't sure I had earned. One winter afternoon. In a beat-up old car. Together on a couch. As close as we ever got to each other.

". . . gentleness," Sam said. "That's what it was. I mean, she was always gentle. But those last weeks when we saw her, there was this way she had with both of us, as if she wanted us to know it was all okay. Everything . . . I can't get it *right*, but it was a kind of . . ."

"Love."

Sam stared into the manicured wealth of Alexandria, Virginia, blinking back tears.

"You're odd, Mr. Eric. Why do people tell you these things?"

"I'm a professional journalist. It's natural."

It was meant to be a joke, but Sam didn't hear me.

"I don't think she thought we needed her anymore. That's wrong, you know. Do you have any kids?"

"A daughter."

"Remember that. It's wrong. It's *always* wrong."

I nodded. A change came over her, desperation rising from somewhere deep and unexpected. Her voice was thick when she spoke.

"Why do you think she did it?"

"I have no idea."

"Yes, you do."

"No."

"You're a surprisingly bad liar, Mr. Eric."

She looked like her mother and she wasn't her mother and would never be her mother, which was the great gift Anna had left her. I wondered what Anna would want me to say. I wondered what words could do her justice.

"I think she had decided a long time ago. I think the only question was when it would be okay—when she could leave and hurt people as little as possible. You and your brother, really. When she thought you could manage without her."

As I said this I saw the truth of it. I saw how Anna had chosen each day to go on, and not just to go on, but to *live*, with all that asks of us, and it seemed to me the bravest thing I had ever seen.

But Sam looked at me in disbelief. "That's horrible. How can you say that? Her whole life—she was just waiting to kill herself? That's *terrible*! I can't believe you're saying that."

"I'm sorry, you don't understand. I'm not saying she was waiting to die. I'm saying she loved every day she lived more than you or I can imagine because she had made a promise to herself a long time ago. She thought she . . ." I stopped because Anna had decided long ago that she didn't want them to know. "Listen. You said how much everything hurt, right? It was like that when I knew her, too. It was always like that and she never made a big deal out of it, but it was always there. And I just think she had made a promise to herself that, when she could, she would end it. The pain. But every day, for years and years, she didn't. Every day she got up and made a choice that this wouldn't be the day, that she would find something to treasure about this day, and that was the thing about her, that was the amazing thing about your mother."

I was scaring Sam and I knew I wasn't getting it right, I wasn't doing Anna justice.

"I don't—"

"Listen to me. You and your brother filled her with more joy than anything else in the world. I'm sure of that. You called me her great love. That's silly. It was you and Stephen and always you and Stephen. I was just some young guy—incredibly charming, no doubt, Sam—but it was you two, you were everything, every day, every moment, *everything*. She treasured them all—every moment with you. She did, in a way you and I can never understand because she had measured them out. She had chosen to give herself a certain number."

This was both true and a lie. I could never know how much I finally meant to Anna, but I knew how much she meant to me, the young man who needed to be taught so many things and then sent on his way. I suddenly saw, as I never had before, what that must have cost her—not letting me go, but letting me get close enough for it to matter.

Sam's attention had turned to the small cemetery. She was trying to decide how much I had hurt and offended her.

"I don't understand, and I think you're probably full of shit. And now you've ruined my brother's wedding."

"I'm sorry."

"I just came out here to say hi and . . ."

"The thing you have to understand is you're not the reason she died. You're the reason she lived."

She shook her head. "Just stop. Please. I can't think about it now."

"I am sorry. I'm not coming to the reception. But tell your brother how much I appreciated being invited."

Squared shoulders and a raised chin and refusal for now to surrender to doubt or confusion, a daughter you would be proud of, Anna. But you were. I know you were.

"Still odd, Mr. Eric. I wish I could say it was good to see you."

Then I was alone with the grass and the stones and the perfect blue sky. The distant murmur of traffic like the fundamental sound of the universe working toward some obscure purpose. Had I done the right thing? Should I have told her more? Is there anything worse, I wondered, than a half-told tale, and do we ever get more than that? Because this is where the story ends, standing outside a church, wondering about all I said or should have said. It was time to go home.

. . .

BUT THERE WAS A DAY I haven't told you about, an unexpectedly warm afternoon in late fall, a last gasp of Indian summer on Veterans Day. Anna had taken pictures of the parade earlier, but we decided to go with commemorative rather than celebratory, so we drove out to the Shannon cemetery, where too many of the graves were staked with flags.

"I love cemeteries," I said, and this was before she had told me anything, really, but all Anna did was smile.

"Is it because there's no one to interrupt you?"

"No, they're great. Peace and quiet. Beautiful grass. Old stone. What's not to like?"

Her smile sat there, delicately balanced, small plastic flags snapping impatiently behind her, and then she was laughing, I know now, at my innocence.

"Nothing," she said. "We should have brought a picnic."

A different season but a beautiful day. Like this one. She knelt in the grass and took pictures while I read the names and dates on the tombstones, sometimes aloud. A hundred endings etched in stone and the ghosts all dispelled, as harmless as the scattered clouds sailing high above us. My father had died a few months earlier and another winter was coming for Anna, but we were momentarily free of it all. I remember her lowering the lens and listening as I read some strange family history revealed in stone. I think it was three wives and twelve children, with the epitaph, "Devoted father and husband," and I had intoned "and husband and husband . . ." And I remember Anna's laughter, always surprisingly loud and sensual, and there was nothing more complicated than this: the two of us in a field of grass and cut stone on the last perfect day of autumn, and friendship, affection, love, use whatever word you're comfortable with. They're all true.

"Well," Anna said, running her finger along the carved words. "You have to live, right?"

You do. You did.

Look at us sitting cross-legged in the grass, so young, really, both of us. The trees along the edge of the cemetery are very nearly bare and the wind blows the stray leaves loose and they pinwheel through the air like the days in all the years since, and ours are already so fleeting, but I see you relaxing into this nearly forgotten and perfect day, your tangled hair back, your dark eyes bright, your smile relit every time the sun escapes the clouds. Look at us! We are alive to everything. You reach deep into the grass and toss a handful into the air and it hangs there, blown apart, a tangled alphabet, a story, a life, sure to tumble as all things must, but not now, not yet. It floats above your open palm in the blue sky, like our young hearts, aloft.

ACKNOWLEDGMENTS

I WOULD LIKE TO THANK Starling Lawrence, Ellen Levine, and Leslie Perls for their sensitive and thoughtful readings of this novel. Most of all I would like to thank my wife, Aurelie Sheehan, whose patience and careful attention as I worked my way through earlier drafts of Anna and Eric's story prove that it is, indeed, possible for people to collaborate in both love and work.